The Rancher's Home

SILVER CREEK RANCH
BOOK FIVE

DARIE MCCOY

EDITED BY
ALL THAT'S WRIGHT

ISBN Ebook: 978-1-961999-13-8

Paperback: 978-1-961999-17-6

The Silver Creek Ranch

Forgotten military heroes who needed a helping hand re-entering the society they had been sworn to protect. The Silver Creek Ranch provided a space where these cowboys could work the land and get back in touch with the men they once were.

The battles of war left scars on each of them.

Healing was what these cowboys needed.

Who knew it would comprise the touch, kiss, and love of a good woman?

The Silver Creek Ranch is an interracial cowboy romance shared world. Each captivating story is filled with plenty of heat and will leave your heart racing with the desire to devour every one of them.

The Rancher's Home

When home is more than a place.

Former Army Ranger Rothschild 'Roth' Stephens has found comforting peace in the vast, tranquil expanse of his Texas ranch. Scarred both physically and emotionally from his time in the service, Roth prefers his own quiet company, filling his days with the grueling, rhythmic chores of ranch life.

Autumn Daley, a successful corporate attorney, has spent years burying herself in work to escape the haunting memories of her past. However, her work life has become untenable. Circumstances bring her home where she faces old memories, along with the man who witnessed the most horrible day of her life. Roth Stephens. Her brother's best friend.

When they meet again, they both attempt to ignore their draw to one another. However, Autumn is forced to seek Roth's help. The sparks they'd tried to deny existed, ignite. What starts as a simple favor soon evolves into a deeper connection as they confront their pasts and navigate the complexities of their emotions.

Roth finds a different kind of peace with Autumn. But, can he hold on to it? What will it take for them to realize the home they seek is with each other?

For those who are still trying to find their home.

"A lost soul can always be found in the refuge of love, where the heart knows its true home."

— UNKNOWN

Prologue

Autumn sat on the tufted bench avoiding making eye contact with herself in the mirror on the vanity. She knew what she'd see and wasn't sure she was ready to face it. Tears pooled in her eyes before dripping down her cheeks when a strangled sob escaped.

It was her wedding day. She was supposed to be happy. Any tears she shed should be from the joy of marrying the man she loved. Instead, she was trying to figure out how she could go through with marrying Russell knowing what she knew. After seeing him in the arms of someone else, professing his love and telling the woman nothing between them would change.

The previous night

The nerves, which had sent her to Russell's place to see him, morphed into something completely different when the woman turned in his embrace, giving Autumn a clear view of her face. At the same moment Autumn recognized her, the woman became aware of Autumn's presence. Her eyes widened marginally before her lips stretched into a smile.

"Russell, baby. We have company."

Further crushing her heart, Russell's face scrunched into a scowl once he noticed Autumn standing there.

"Autumn, what the fuck are you doing here? Aren't you supposed to be with your bridesmaids?"

Instead of answering him, Autumn fired back her own question. "Is this why you didn't want a Bachelor party? So, you and your 'cousin' could do...whatever it is you two are doing?"

Autumn put air quotes around the word cousin. Because, unless they were the kissing kind, there was no way Russell was related to Lucy as he'd told her in the beginning of their relationship. Autumn had been leery of dating the upper classman and had taken notice of Lucy always seeming to be in his orbit. Russell had laughed off Autumn's concern, assuring her there was nothing between the two of them except for a close family relation.

The fact that the two looked nothing alike could be easily explained since Autumn had cousins she shared no obvious familial features with. Not everyone's relatives were cookie cutter replicas of each other.

"It doesn't matter why I didn't want a party. **You** said **you did**. So, why are you here instead of with them?"

Tears clouded Autumn's vision, and she swiped at them, staring at Russell in disbelief.

"Are you seriously going to act like you weren't just tonguing Lucy down? That you weren't telling her nothing between you two would change once we got married? How could you do this to me, Russ?"

Russell's handsome face was a mask of fury. "I didn't do anything to you. You did it to yourself when you decided to show up here unannounced. All of this could've been avoided if you'd stayed your ass where you were supposed to be."

Autumn was almost too stunned to speak. Was he truly blaming her? His words fully penetrated, and she was nearly bowled over at the implication. He wasn't even slightly ashamed *of what he was doing. He was simply annoyed she'd complicated things by finding out.*

Slowly, Autumn started backing away, shaking her head. She had to. If she'd stayed where she was, she was going to completely fly into a rage and destroy everything in her path—including the two of them. Especially the two of them.

"I can't do this. I won't do this."

Autumn pushed the words past the cotton and gravel lodged in her throat. She could barely breathe. Hurt and anger had control of her basic autonomous functions.

"What do you mean you can't do this?"

The entire time he'd been talking to her, Russell hadn't budged from his position next to Lucy, with her practically plastered against him. That is until Autumn made her declaration. Then, he none-too-gently set Lucy aside as his long legs covered the distance between them in a few strides.

Jerking away when he attempted to touch her, Autumn shook her head again.

"No. Don't touch me. I don't want your hands on me, and I don't want to hear anything you have to say."

Alarms were blaring in her head, telling her to get away. Encouraging her not to listen to a lying word coming from Russell's deceitful mouth. Autumn couldn't explain why she didn't keep going. Why she stopped. Why she allowed him to say even one word. But she did.

Present

Autumn could no longer avoid her own reflection. Staring into her red eyes, she took note of her puffy eyelids and the red splotches on her face from her crying jag. Why had she listened to Russell? Why did she let him get to her, reminding her of all the people who'd been invited to the wedding? Her extended family, her parent's professional connections. The people who hadn't just driven an hour to see her get married, they'd gotten on planes and rented hotel rooms for the occasion.

Not to mention all the money her parents spent on the venue and the million other things which were a requirement for someone of their social standing to have at their wedding. With her parent's wealth, one would think the money spent wouldn't be something that could sway Autumn. But, she hadn't been raised to be careless with how she spent it. Besides, it wasn't just the wedding. Since Autumn was fresh out of college with her bachelor's degree, and Russell was in his first year of practice after law school, her parents had purchased them a starter home as a wedding present.

How could she look them in the eyes and tell them she'd failed? At the thought, the tears she'd bitten back started up again. A few soft taps to the door had her wiping her face and attempting to sit up straighter. She'd managed to keep her mother and the others at bay, but her temporary reprieve was apparently over.

"Tummy, is everything okay, baby girl?"

Her father's voice coming from the other side of the heavy door wasn't what Autumn expected to hear. She fully assumed it was her mother looking to encourage her to let the make-up artist and hair stylist inside to start getting her ready. She was already more than a half hour behind schedule.

However, hearing her father's voice brought her tears out in earnest, a sob ripped from her throat as she nearly folded herself in half on the bench seat. She couldn't even form the words to answer him, but she needn't have worried. Autumn suddenly went from nearly lying on the vanity seat to being cradled in her father's arms as if she was five again and had awakened from a nightmare. Well, she wasn't five, but this experience was most assuredly a nightmare.

It took some coaxing, gentle reassurance, and the patience her father was known for to get Autumn to do more than paint his shirt and jacket with her tears. When she'd spilled the whole sordid tale, he nodded as he rubbed her back. After telling him, Autumn felt so much lighter. As if keeping everything to herself was an anvil around her neck. Telling her father cut the chain tying it to her.

"Autumn Marianne Daley."

Autumn sat up straight, staring at her father with wide eyes. He'd used her full name. He *never* used her full name. Her throat clogged again as she waited for what he'd say next.

"You are my child. I don't care how much money has been spent. I don't care if I leveraged myself to my eyeballs to pay for this shit—which I didn't—I'd never expect you to tie yourself to a piece of shit man who can't do right by you. Not simply to please me. Not to please *anyone*."

Relief flooded every fiber of Autumn's being. As ashamed as she was of the situation Russell put her in, she was more ashamed she hadn't dismissed any concerns and remembered who her parents were. They had always assured her and her older brother, Nicholas, they wanted them to be happy— above all else. Her parents would never ask her to sacrifice herself to save face.

"Now, answer me this. Is this what *you* want? Do you still want to marry that piece of shit—I mean...Russell. Do you still want to marry Russell?"

"No, sir. I don't. But—"

"No buts, Tummy." Standing, he held out his hand. "Come with me."

Unsure of what her father's next move would be, Autumn put her hand in his. When he opened the door, her mother, aunt, and a couple of cousins almost fell inside the room. Smoothing away imaginary wrinkles in her dress, her mother swept her gaze over Autumn.

"Autumn, baby. Why aren't you dressed? And your hair is a mess."

"Carla, stop." Her mother's gaze whipped to her father's

face. In a succinct, ask-me-no-questions, tone her father informed his wife that the wedding was off.

Her mother's mouth worked like a fish processing water before she sputtered, "Travis? What do you mean? Why?"

All her father did was shake his head before saying softly, "We'll talk about it later. Can you tell the wedding coordinator so they can inform the guests and get a message out?"

Not waiting for an answer, he tugged Autumn through the outer room and into the hallway. A short distance away from the door was Nicholas, standing next to his best friend, Roth. The two were on leave from the military. Even in regular civilian suits, the way they stood, with their straight backs and squared shoulders, was a giveaway to their association with the armed forces.

Roth noticed them first. His face was normally open and friendly, but a hard mask slid into place before he tapped Nick alerting him to their presence. Her brother stopped talking. When he looked at her face, his expression shifted to match his friend's.

"What's going on, Pops?" Nick peered at their father after his inspection of Autumn's face.

"The wedding is off."

Nick immediately looked back at Autumn. "What did that fucker do to you?"

Autumn would've gasped at Nick cursing in front of their father, but knew he'd get a pass based on the situation. When she didn't answer him quickly enough, Nick returned his stare to their father, who was more than happy to supply the details he hadn't given her mother.

The next few moments were surreal as she learned where her father was taking her with Nick and Roth following closely behind. She didn't have complete clarity until he shoved the door open to the room where Russell was waiting with his groomsmen.

With her father, brother, and Roth standing at her back, Autumn told Russell again she wouldn't marry him. Only this time, he couldn't guilt her into going through with it. Needless to say, he didn't take it well. The second the first insult fell from Russell's lips, her father guided her to the door. He pushed her out and locked it behind her before she could see more than Roth using the front of Russell's pristinely pressed suit to lift him from the floor.

Chapter One

Roth put the ATV in park, then pushed his hat upwards with the tip of his finger, releasing a sigh. Looking toward the front stairs of the ranch house, he exhaled before climbing out of the vehicle. Once he did, it was hard to miss the helicopter on the pad a short distance away from the house.

"What happened?" His already deep voice was gruff as he approached his oldest brother, Ryker.

"Why does something have to happen for me to come see my little brother?"

Roth grunted. He was only two years younger, but Ryker insisted on calling him and Rhinehart his little brothers. Sure, he was the tallest by a whole inch, but there was nothing little about the Stephens boys, as they'd been called as long as he could remember. Ryker stood at six-foot-six inches while Roth and Rhine topped out at six-foot-five inches. All three had wide shoulders, barrel chests, and thick bodies. So, being called little wasn't something Roth associated with either of them.

Stepping closer to where his brother stood on the top

stair, leaning against one column, Roth arched a single eyebrow.

"You didn't take a copter ride just to come sit on my porch and shoot the breeze. You call for that."

Stopping once he was abreast of his eldest sibling, Roth stared at him. "So... What happened?"

"I'm getting married."

"That's old news, brother. You've been engaged for more than a year now."

Shooting him an irritated glance, Ryker flipped him off before stalking over to one of the custom rockers and plopping into it. Lifting his hands, Roth raised both eyebrows.

"What? Am I wrong? Didn't you and Ensley get engaged more than a year ago?"

"Fuck you." Ryker looked off before returning his stare to Roth. "And yes, it's been more than a year. That being said, we've set a date."

Lowering himself into the chair closet to the one Ryker occupied, Roth nodded.

"Good for you. What's the date?" Removing his hat, Roth hung it on his knee before leaning back into the seat.

"October twenty-fifth."

With another bob of his head, Roth acknowledged Ryker's statement.

"I'll put it on my calendar. What do you need me to do?"

Roth had been in a couple of weddings over the years with his army buddies, but Ryker was the first of his siblings to tie the knot.

"I'll have my assistant send you the information. We're having it in Las Vegas. Ensley doesn't know many people in Houston and she doesn't want to have it in her home town. Nothing there is large enough to accommodate us anyway."

"How big of a wedding are you two having?" Roth was genuinely curious. Ryker had a small circle of friends, but a plethora of associates. Ensley appeared to be equally selective in her friend group from what Roth could tell when they'd met and during the times Ryker spoke of her.

As far as family went, he knew Ryker wouldn't blink about flying people out to attend. Although most wouldn't ask, they'd simply be happy to be invited. Many of them were starting to believe Roth and his brothers would never settle down and start families. So, they'd all want to be front row for the occasion.

Gently setting his chair to rocking, Ryker looked over at Roth and shrugged.

"You know if it was up to me, there would be enough people to witness and everyone else would read about it in the paper. But Mama..."

Ryker trailed off. He didn't have to fill in the rest of the sentence. Roth already knew. Their mother was hell bent on getting them married to get her grandbabies. Hell, he knew for a fact she'd been encouraging Ryker and Ensley to get to the baby-making, even if they hadn't tied the knot. And for his Sunday School Teacher mother, that told of her desperation.

"Yeah...Mama is gonna want everybody to see and hear about it. Especially those old biddies who've been throwing their legion of rug rats in her face all these years."

The slow rock of Ryker's chair came to an abrupt halt. Roth glanced over to see the stricken expression on his brother's face.

"What? Why do you look like we asked you to give a speech in your skivvies?"

"You don't think she plans to invite all of her judgmental so-called friends do you? I like less than half of them, and it's touch and go with the other half."

Roth shook his head. Tapping his fingertips against the brim of his hat he lifted a shoulder.

"You never know with her. You know how she is. The first

of her sons getting married is a major event. I'm surprised she didn't strong arm you into having it in Lone Star Ridge, if you didn't want to do Houston."

"If we aren't having it in the little one stoplight town Ensley's from, why would I have it here? Lone Star Ridge isn't much bigger than Piney Bend, Mississippi."

Throwing his hands up in surrender, Roth tilted his head toward Ryker.

"Don't get testy with me. I'm just making an observation. It's your wedding. You can have it wherever you want. I'm good with it not being in Lone Star. Hell, Mama would probably try to get me to pitch fancy tents and all kinds of shit to have it here on the ranch. No thank you to having more than half the town and a shit-ton of strangers trapsing around all over my land. It makes the cows nervous."

Ryker's posture relaxed halfway through Roth's speech, and he began nodding in agreement. There was no way in hell Roth was having any type of event on his ranch. He intentionally didn't do crowds. He was never too fond of them, but after his last deployment before leaving the Army, things got pretty bad.

It took him years, and some time working with Andy Harvey on the Silver Creek Ranch, to get to where he could sporadically attend large gatherings. *Very sporadically*. He preferred the company of the animals on the ranch and the camaraderie with the ranch hands who worked it with him. There were less than twenty of them, and most didn't live on the ranch in the bunkhouses he provided.

His issue with big crowds was likely the reason Ryker felt he needed to come speak to him personally. Roth would have to prep himself for being in Las Vegas—especially the part where he'd have to be enclosed in a room with a bunch of people.

"I'm sure you're really worried about the cows." Ryker leveled him with a look filled with the same sarcasm coating his voice.

"What? They're sensitive beasts." Roth's additional rebuttal died on his lips when the screen door pushed open and his housekeeper stepped out onto the porch.

"Here." Amelia Blake shoved a cellphone in his direction.

"What're you giving me this for?" Accepting the phone, which looked nothing like his, he stared up at her.

"Because you aren't answering yours, Miss Ginny has taken to calling me." Turning on her heel, Amelia went back into the house with the same flourish she'd used to exit.

Before putting the device to his ear, Roth gave Ryker a questioning glance. Shaking his head, his brother answered the silent query.

"Don't ask me. She didn't mention your name when I was there earlier."

Lifting the device, Roth tried to avoid getting his finger tangled up in the strap of the wallet case Amelia had the thing wrapped in.

"Hey, Mama. What's going on?"

"Why does something have to be going on for me to call?"

One corner of Roth's lips tipped up in a knowing smirk, then he responded. "Because, Mama. If you're calling me on Amelia's phone, it means you've been trying to call mine. That kinda determination means something has happened. But, since you're not leading with it, I'm guessing it's nothing life threatening."

"Of course not! If you'd picked up or answered my texts, this wouldn't be necessary."

His mother had the audacity to sound affronted that he'd even suggest she'd overstepped by calling his housekeeper's cellphone in an effort to reach him.

"Okay then, Mama. What can I do for you?"

"Well, you know how I've been a member of the Ladies' Auxiliary for years. I finally talked them into doing something worthwhile, and we're having a fundraiser."

Roth's brow dipped. Something was suspicious, but he went with it.

"That sounds nice, Mama. Let me know your goal, and I'll be sure to make a donation. Do you want me to tell Ryker and Rhine? Ryker's right here."

Ryker shot him a glare before immediately standing from the rocking chair. Roth's hand was already up to block the swipe he knew his brother was going to take at his head when he walked by. In his ear, his mother obliviously replied.

"Oh, no. Don't bother. I know he's gonna donate, because he can't participate. Not with him being engaged and all. Not unless I can somehow get Ensley involved. And I don't think that'll happen in a million years."

Picking up on a few key words, Roth's frown deepened. "Mama, why would Ensley need to be involved for Ryker to participate?"

"Because, silly. It's a charity auction. We're calling it, Hearts for Heroes. Isn't that cute?"

The mention of a charity auction got his full attention. His back stiffened and he sat ramrod straight in his seat. He loved his mama, but there was no way in hell he was parading around in front of a bunch of strangers to raise money. His check would have to be good enough.

"Yeah, Mama. It's cute, but the answer is no. I'm not peacocking for a bunch of strangers. Not even for charity."

"Pardon my grits? I don't recall asking you to do any such thing. For your information, it's dates with eligible women being auctioned—not men. As handsome as all my sons are, I don't think I can get anyone to bid on either one of you ornery so-and-sos. You're too much like your daddy."

"Mama, you married our daddy."

"Did I ask you who I married?"

If her tone of voice was any indicator, Virginia Stephens was getting tired of Roth's commentary. He wisely opted not to respond to her retort.

"Anyway, as I was saying, the women have graciously volunteered to go on dates with the highest bidders. Of course, the terms are clear that nothing more than spending time with said woman should be expected. We're the Ladies' Auxiliary, not madams. We aren't selling *s-e-x*."

Not only did his mother spell the word, she whispered when she did it. Roth exercised supreme effort to hold in his laughter. He wouldn't be the one to tell her he knew all about sex, and it wasn't necessary for her to do either thing when talking to him about it.

"Okay. So, if you don't need me to be in it, what do you need? Like I said, I'm happy to donate. I can write you a check first thing."

"I don't want your check, Rothschild. I want to see you there. To bid on a date with a pretty lady. That's how you can show your support, by showing your face at my event."

"Mama..."

"Did I mention that the charity we're supporting is geared toward veterans? I know how important it is to you to help your fellow veterans re-enter society after serving their country."

That was below the belt, but it appeared his mama was prepared to pull out all the stops to get her way.

"Did I mention, Carla said Nick would be home, and he's going to be there too?"

Oh, she was really digging deep by bringing up his best friend of more than thirty years. Nick was still active duty, but he claimed he was going to retire soon. Either way, if he'd managed time off, there was no way Roth was going to get out of at least showing his face. Heaving a disgruntled sigh, Roth slumped back into his seat.

"Okay, Mama. When is this shindig?"

Chapter Two

Autumn couldn't believe she'd let her mother guilt her into filling in at the last minute for this charity auction for the Ladies' Auxiliary. If she saw her cousin Vivienne anytime soon, she was gonna box her ears. How could she put her in such a position? For that matter, how could her mother agree to such a thing? Being sold to the highest bidder wasn't something that appealed to Autumn in the least.

No matter what they called it, it was sale. They could say it was a date, but it reeked of flesh peddling—especially with the way the women in question were parading around in their most elegant tramp attire. Autumn was no slut-shamer, but they looked like they were selling more than a couple of hours of their time. Looking down at herself, her floor length, shimmery rose gold evening gown looked like a nun's habit in comparison. Which was saying something, because her girls were sitting up nicely with more cleavage than she liked being on display by the vee in the neckline.

"Stop looking like you're ready to run for the door at any second." Her mother's admonishment was whispered in Autumn's ear.

When she pulled back, wearing an indulgent smile, no one would ever guess she'd been chastising her only daughter. If anything, they would think she was giving her a compliment. Returning a smile nearly as fake, Autumn tried one more time to convince her mother to simply let her write a check.

"Mama, are you sure I can't just make a donation? I'll bet it would get the charity more money than whatever someone might bid on me."

"Tut-tut, Autumn. Shush it. First of all, we need ten bachelorettes. If you drop out, we won't have enough. Second, are you insinuating *my* daughter isn't stunning enough to inspire these wealthy men to give generously in the hopes of winning an evening with you?"

"An evening? Why would the date have to be at night?" Autumn couldn't wipe the horrified expression from her face. "Besides, Mama, I'm not here permanently. I'm on sabbatical. I haven't quit my job and moved back to Lone Star Ridge."

Flicking her fingers as if she were waving away a pesky insect, her mother shook her head.

"I told you; every bidder was informed the date had to be approved by the young lady. So, you can set the terms. Stop being so dramatic."

"I'm not being dramatic. I'm just not keen on being some lecherous old man's date."

"Girl, stop it! There are plenty of young men here with pockets deep enough to pledge a nice sized donation to spend time with you."

Swatting at Autumn, her mother wasn't able to suppress her giggle. They both knew Autumn wasn't exaggerating about the lecherous old men. Their most recent conversations had included Autumn's lamenting of continuing to be the object of many a man over sixty-five's attention. And while she still thought of both her parents as vibrant, being involved with someone thirty years her senior wasn't Autumn's idea of a good time.

The problem was, she fell into the age range where the primary men who displayed interest in her were either old enough to be her father or young enough to be her son. There was no in between. When someone in her age range expressed interest, it usually lasted long enough for them to realize she actually used her own brain. So, she wasn't a fit for them. Translation. They couldn't dominate her the way they wanted, so they moved on.

Despite her mother's assurances, Autumn didn't hold out hope of being saved. Her mother had already nixed the idea of Nick bidding on her. So, she couldn't even ask her brother to bail her out of it. Speaking of whom, where had he gotten off to? Scanning the room, Autumn smiled politely when she accidentally made eye contact with any of the aforementioned, undesirable, potential bidders.

She had to admit, the ladies had transformed the Lone Star Ridge community center into an elegant venue. She'd thought they would move the event to Houston in order to have it in a classy ballroom in one of the major hotels. But, they'd managed to pull it off. They even made the small stage look like something from a fairy tale garden—gazebo style for the ladies to stand during the bidding.

When she finally located Nick, Autumn's heart lodged in her throat. He was standing next to Rothschild Stephens. Of course, he'd abandon them when he linked up with his best friend. The two were near one of the stand-up tables with the wall at their backs. Neither looked pleased to be there, but Roth appeared particularly uncomfortable.

"Mama, I'm gonna go talk to Nick and Roth."

Before she could make it more than a step, her mother grasped her wrist. Turning, Autumn gave her a questioning stare.

"Yes, ma'am?"

"Now, we've been jokie-ha-ha, but I'm serious. Don't you go over there trying to pressure your brother into bidding on you."

"I'm not, Mama." Autumn put as much sincerity in her expression as she could manage. "I promise."

"Mhm." Her mother delivered a curt nod, then let go of her wrist. "I need to find my husband anyway. If I leave him alone too long, he'll eat everything he's not supposed to then complain to me later about his ailments."

Autumn was stopped no less than three times on her quest to join Nick and Roth. She had absolutely no intention of breaking her promise to her mother. There would be no need, if Plan B worked out.

"Hey, y'all." Autumn's smile was wide as she approached them.

"Aw, hell. I need a fresh drink." Nick shook his head, then side stepped her on his way to the bar on the other side of the room.

"Wait! Why are you leaving? I didn't say anything but, hey."

Continuing to back away, Nick's expression said he didn't believe her. He confirmed it when he spoke.

"Nope. I know that smile. Whatever it is, I want no part in it."

"Nick!"

Remembering her mother's lessons about decorum, the smile never slid from Autumn's face as she whisper-hissed at her retreating brother. When she finally turned back toward Roth, he was leaning against the wall with his arms folded across his chest. His expression was unreadable, but somehow still managed to project intensity.

"Heeeyy, Roth."

Although Roth's responding nod was his only acknowledgement of her greeting, Autumn pasted on her most sincere smile as she moved closer to him. She stopped about a foot away, placing her beaded clutch onto the table before resting her forearm on the surface. Not wanting their conversation to be overheard, she glanced over her shoulder before angling her body so she could see both him and the rest of the room better.

She immediately wished she hadn't been so diligent. Standing two tables away was Vilmer Cartwright. The man wasn't a day under seventy-five, which was three years older than her father. And while she thought her dad a handsome and fit man, she didn't consider men in his age range potential dating material.

There was only so far she was willing go to for charity. Fending off a rich, handsy, grandfather wasn't anywhere on her list. Despite what her mother said, she knew moneyed men like Cartwright didn't participate in activities like this for the sake of giving to a good cause. They had other ways to get their tax write-offs.

He lifted his champagne glass in her direction before she quickly averted her eyes. When her gaze returned to Roth, a small frown line had appeared between his eyebrows.

"What do you want, Tummy?"

Autumn had to work not to grimace when he called her by the nickname her family used. It started as a cute way to acknowledge her rounded belly as a baby and play off her name. The nickname had stuck, even into Autumn's thirties. While she had long gotten over her teenage crush on her brother's best friend, something about hearing him call her Tummy, grated on her. Maybe because it made her feel like the awkward twelve-year-old she was when she realized Roth wasn't simply her brother's friend who was nice to her. He was seriously hot.

Where she'd used to chatter almost non-stop whenever he

came over to hang out with Nick, she'd suddenly began stumbling over her words and forgetting how to form coherent sentences. When he took her back there, she always needed a moment to regroup. She had to remind herself she was very much an adult and no longer a slave to her hormonal crushes.

Tapping his folded arms with her fingertips, Autumn kept her smile bright.

"Don't be like that, Roth."

"Tummy..." The warning in his voice was accompanied by the lowering of his brow when he tilted his head down, piercing her with a penetrating stare.

Uncaring about her mother's lessons on ladylike behavior, Autumn sucked her teeth. She barely managed to refrain from stomping her foot in frustration.

"Okay, fine. You have to help me."

"Help you with what?" Unfolding his arms, Roth's expression shifted, giving Autumn a sliver of hope.

"You know what this thing is about. And while I believe the cause they're supporting is worthy, I didn't sign up to fight off unwanted advances from men I'd never date on purpose. I need someone I can trust to win the date."

Roth's head projected his answer before he spoke, dashing the shard of optimism Autumn was clinging to.

"Nope. I'm going home in exactly fifteen minutes. I will have been here a solid hour at that point and fulfilled my obligation. I showed my face. I plan to leave before any of that starts."

Autumn's heart landed in her stomach. Not bothering to take a cursory glance around the room, she stepped closer to Roth. The material of his tuxedo jacket felt heavy beneath her fingertips. Her grip was as desperate as the ball of dread building inside her.

"You can't leave! Mama won't let me bid on myself, she's

forbidden Nick to do it, and you know no one here has the balls to bid against Mr. Cartwright. You *have* to buy me!"

Roth's dark amber eyes were shielded by his unfairly long eyelashes as he looked from her face to where her hand rested on his arm, then back to her face. Internally, Autumn gulped, but kept her stare firmly on him while she tried to ignore the firm muscles beneath her fingers and the heat wafting from his large body.

"Tummy... Sugar, have you thought about how it will look for me to *buy* you?" The air quotes around the word buy were implied in his tone.

A small line appeared between her eyebrows, and Autumn's head rocked back a little. Glazing over the endearment, she focused on his reasoning for saying no.

"Roth, I'm a black woman at a charity auction where I've been asked to parade across a stage to be assessed for how much money they want to spend on me. Of course I have. How is it better for some dirty old white man to buy me? At least you're a member of the same generation as me, and I won't have to fight you to keep your hands to yourself."

"How do you know I'm not a dirty, young white man?"

Autumn tapped his solid forearm, then squeezed it. "Stop playing, Roth. Are you going to help me or do I have to be low down and remind you of all the care packages and letters I sent you while you were deployed? The Christmas presents for you and your guys..."

Roth's expression went through another shift before he lifted one eyebrow and grumbled. "It seems like you don't have a problem going there."

She hadn't wanted to do it, but if the big guns were necessary to make sure she stayed out of the crosshairs of Vilmer Cartwright, she'd use them. If he were a kind man, she wouldn't have a problem, but he creeped her out. There was no way her mother would expect her to honor a date with him, but her mother was also under the delusion some of the younger wealthy men present would bid on her.

Autumn concluded that her mother's love blinded her to her daughter's reality. So, Autumn really needed Plan B to work. Giving Roth her most pitiful, big-eyed pleading look, she bit her bottom lip while staring at him.

"Shit... Fine. I'll bid on you. Just stop looking at me like that, Sugar."

The flip-flop in her belly and the flutter of her lady bits were hard to ignore, but Autumn managed as her lips stretched into a wide smile. Ignoring his shift to calling her *Sugar*, she bounced excitedly.

"Thank you, Roth. You won't regret it. I can transfer the money to you. So, you don't even really have to come out of your own pocket."

"Did I say I needed your money?"

Autumn immediately picked up on the change in his demeanor, and quickly tried to make amends.

"I'm sorry, Roth. I was just trying to say, I didn't expect you to spend your own money to do me a favor. The bidding on these things starts in the five-figure range."

The words kept coming out wrong, but Autumn couldn't stop them. After they hit the air, she knew she wasn't helping her case at all.

"Sugar, stop trying to clean it up. You're just making it worse. I don't need your money. I was planning to donate anyway."

Relief crashed over Autumn. The feeling was short lived. A moment later, there was an announcement for all auction participants to report to the stage. She was frozen in place until Roth placed his hands on her shoulders. Turning her in the direction of the stage, Autumn felt warmth against her back when he leaned close to her ear. His beard tickled her skin as he spoke to her loud enough for only her to hear.

"Go on, Sugar. A promise is a promise. You keep your word, and I'll keep mine."

With Roth's assurance, Autumn threaded her way through the attendees to reach the podium to get her number and take her place in line.

Chapter Three

Twenty minutes prior, Roth had been certain he'd end the night at exactly nine p.m. and take his ass back to the ranch to the peace and quiet he loved. It had taken a long ride and some stall mucking meditation to get his mind right to even attend. The bonus was having his long-time friend, Nick Daley, there to keep him from having to make small talk all evening. Roth nearly shuddered at the thought of engaging in inane conversation with the hoity toity elites of Lone Star Ridge.

If he wasn't such a damn mama's boy, he would be in his chair right now. Hell, even with his mama's boy ways, he'd still have ditched the event early if it wasn't for Autumn strolling over in those fuck-me heels and rip-me-off dress. The fight he'd put up to not participate in the bidding process had nothing to do with not wanting to be involved with the auction and everything to do with him not trusting himself. Not with her.

It had been that way since she'd almost married that walking pile of shit more than ten years ago. Roth leaned against the wall as the Ladies' Auxiliary milled around murmuring in an effort to assemble their bachelorettes. Roth's eyes never left Autumn as he let his mind drift back to the day he'd realized little Tummy wasn't so little anymore.

Past

Roth fought the urge to tug at the collar of the tuxedo. It was a perfect fit, but it still didn't feel as natural to him as wearing his dress blues. Not that being in anything outside of his normal gear or jeans with cowboy boots felt natural. But at least in his military issued gear, he had a purpose. Just like being in his jeans and boots meant he was hard at work on his grandfather's ranch.

Nick wasn't normally a talkative guy. It was part of the reason he and Roth had been friends for so long. They both knew when to shut up. Today, however, Nick was more chatty than usual. He was also filled with ideas which had started out sounding borderline insane to Roth, but were looking better and better the longer they waited to receive the signal to get into position for Autumn's wedding. Like him, Nick's gut said the douchebag Autumn was supposed to marry wasn't worthy of her.

While not many men were, Russell Shack wasn't even in the fifty percentile of possible matches. In Roth's opinion. He'd only admit to himself that his opinion was heavily biased. He and Nick had been best friends ever since they met at the creek serving as the natural border between their grandparents' properties as pre-teens. So, he'd known Autumn for more than half her life.

Her kindness and loyalty shouldn't be wasted on a cow patty like Russell. Roth had zero proof to substantiate his feelings. But, he trusted his gut. To the point he almost agreed to Nick's plan to shove him into a rucksack and drop him off in the desert. The second he saw Mr. Daley approaching with Autumn at his side, the plan didn't sound the least bit crazy.

Autumn's beautiful face held red splotches to match the puffy redness surrounding her normally sparkling brown eyes. Instantly, Roth was on alert. Halting Nick's most recent sugges-

tion, he alerted him to their presence. Somehow, Roth managed to camouflage the relief he felt when Mr. Daley said the wedding was off.

Nick beat Roth in asking what the fucker had done to her. There was no question Russell was at fault. Autumn was what he'd heard her mother describe as nose-wide-open in love with Russell. If she'd decided to call off the wedding the day of, he'd done something majorly fucked up.

As he listened to Mr. Daley, Roth's anger grew. He watched Autumn, seeing the hurt bordering on devastation in her demeanor. Even if he was hearing the reasons his immediate dislike of her former fiancé was justified, Roth didn't revel in the knowledge. It brought her pain, which made it wholly unacceptable.

His fingers flexed as he exchanged a glance with Nick as they followed Mr. Daley and Autumn to the room where Russell and his groomsmen were waiting before the wedding. Both he and Nick had avoided the room since their dislike of Russell wasn't a secret.

The second they stepped into the room Roth began assessing the potential skill of the other men present. Most weren't the physical type and were more likely to pull out their cellphones to record or call for help than they were to jump into the fray. After Autumn told the douche the wedding was off, Roth's muscles coiled in preparation for action.

Technically, he could land in the brig for even half of the things he'd considered doing to Russell, but potential punishment didn't matter when the asshole opened his mouth and insulted Autumn. Whatever he'd planned to say after calling her dumb and disparaging her weight was silenced by Roth's hand at his collar cutting off his oxygen supply.

A cacophony of yells and expletives hit the air as Roth rammed his fist into Russell's pretty face, loosening at least two of his teeth. The other man batted at Roth's arms trying to regain the ability to breathe freely, but Roth wasn't inclined to oblige.

"Please, man."

"Now you know manners?" Roth growled. "No. You don't deserve oxygen if all you know to do with it is run your mouth. Who the fuck do you think you are talking to her like that?"

Roth didn't actually want an answer, and Russell couldn't give him one because he was otherwise occupied with turning blue. The hold Roth had on Russell's collar was only relinquished so he could gain the appropriate leverage to punch him in the stomach, causing the asshole to bend at the waist. At which point, Roth promptly kneed him in the face, knocking him into unconsciousness.

When he finally looked up, there were a couple of other groaning bodies on the floor with the asshole's, and Nick was standing at Roth's back. Mr. Daley was on the opposite side of the small room collecting the cellphones of the non-combative members of the douchebag's little entourage.

Looking down at Russell's prone body, Roth resisted the urge to kick him for good measure. Instead, he met Nick's extended fist, bumping his knuckles. Once he was done with his phone collecting, Mr. Daley joined them. Gesturing to the moaning and unconscious dung piles on the floor, he glanced at the groomsmen.

"You boys clean up this mess, and get them out of here."

"What about our phones, sir?" The bravest in the group ventured to ask, earning himself a glare from Mr. Daley.

"What phones?" Mr. Daley's reply was clear.

When it looked like the guy was going to say something else, one of the others elbowed him in the side.

"Yessir. We'll get this cleaned up."

"Make sure that you do." Mr. Daley placed a hand on Roth and Nick's shoulders. "Come on. Let's get out of here."

~

Present

Roth was snapped back into the present by his mother's voice. Reluctantly, he swung his gaze from Autumn to the woman who birthed him. The one who'd also coerced him into a suit and a room full of people when he'd rather be on his front porch listening to the calming sounds the ranch made at night.

"Okay, everyone. Thank you for your patience. Also, please join me in a round of applause to thank the lovely bachelorettes who've agreed to participate in tonight's event."

Roth kept his eyes on his mother as Nick rejoined him at the stand-up table. *Shit.* In all the back and forth with Autumn, he'd allowed himself to forget about what his friend might think of his agreement to *buy* his sister. Roth still winced at the term in relation to Autumn.

"She talked you into getting her out of this mess, didn't she?" Roth's head snapped around at Nick's statement.

"You knew?"

"Nope. I guessed. She tried to get me to talk to Mama to get her out of it altogether. When she walked over, I figured it didn't work, and she was gonna try to get one of us to throw her a lifeline."

Roth stared at his friend in disbelief. "It doesn't bother you?"

Nick shrugged. "Why would you helping Autumn avoid going on a date with some rando bother me? Besides, it's for charity right? We're both gonna donate to help out either way."

Roth wasn't sure if he should be in awe of Nick's confidence in him or check his latest cognitive eval to see if he was still in peak condition. It took Roth a moment for understanding to smack him in the head like a bucking bull after it kicked him into the air. Nick thought he would simply bid on Autumn without following through with all of the conditions of the auction.

Once the thought was rooted in his mind. He wondered about it himself. What did he plan to do once he won the privilege of sharing a few hours with Autumn Daley? Could he simply let the opportunity slip through his fingers? *Should* he? A lot had changed over the years. He hadn't seen her in more than a passing fashion since before he left the army. She'd moved away for law school after the wedding debacle, and had decided to make Las Vegas her new home when she graduated and passed the bar.

He was so fucked up after he got out of the military, he'd been next to useless until he heard about the Silver Creek Ranch. The time in South Dakota with Andy and the other soldiers going through similar struggles had been what he'd needed. It healed him in a way talking to his VA shrink hadn't. But, it kept him away from family and friends for a long time. When his grandfather's trusted foreman said he couldn't handle the day to day of the ranch anymore, Roth came home. The place was technically his anyway.

Neither Ryker nor Rhine were interested in ranching life. Knowing that, his grandpa had willed the majority ownership to him, giving his brothers small shares. Not enough to overrule his decisions, but enough for them to receive dividends.

Roth realized he hadn't actually responded to Nick's question about Autumn. However, the start of the actual auction saved him from having to continue the conversation. The first young woman was strutting across the stage like she was vying for Miss Texas. His mother aided the woman's pageant presentation by starting the bidding.

"First we have the lovely Miss Scarlett Monroe. Miss Monroe is a recent Longhorn graduate looking to enter post graduate studies in the fall. That is unless some lucky fella snatches her up first and gets her mind on home-making instead."

Roth leaned against the wall and folded his arms once more as he waited for Autumn's number to be called. At present, she stood in the line with a circular badge attached to the bodice of her dress boasting her number in the lineup. Six. He had to sit through this process five more times before he could put them both out of their misery.

"What happened to feminism?" Nick grumbled as he took his place next to him.

Cocking an eyebrow, Roth shot him a glance. "Since when are you a feminist?"

Shrugging, Nick kept his gaze on the stage. "I've always been in favor of women's rights. Having a female soldier pull my ass out of a sling more than once just helped the case."

Roth had to agree with him there. Some of the best soldiers he knew were women. Still, he didn't think his mother had completely gotten the memo about marriage not being every woman's ultimate goal.

"Are you gonna go tell my mama she should encourage Miss Monroe to forget about a ring and go on to graduate school?"

"Fuck no. I'm hoping both of our mothers forget I'm even here."

Roth's chuckle sounded more like a grunt as he returned to watching Autumn. Only this time, when he looked in her direction, she was staring back at him.

Chapter Four

Autumn was on the verge of snatching the corsage shaped button from her chest and tossing it to the floor. *This was stupid*. Not the charity itself. Raising funds to help veterans reintegrate into society was a very worthy cause. In her opinion, not enough was being done for them. So, their ultimate goal was admirable, but this auction was archaic. However, who could tell that to the Ladies' Auxiliary of Lone Star Ridge? Apparently, not Autumn Daley.

"Our next lovely bachelorette is a hometown girl who moved to the big city of sin in Nevada. But, she's back here with us, for a little while at least. Miss Autumn Daley."

Initially, Autumn startled upon hearing her name. Recovering quickly, she pasted a smile on her face, accepted the hand of the usher helping everyone onto the stage, and strode to the spot on the floor where they'd been directed to stand. Unlike the women who went before her, she didn't treat the stage like a runway.

There was no way she was going to turn around and show anyone her ass, no matter how spectacular it looked. She had to admit, the way her dress gently hugged her curves showcased her posterior to perfection. Autumn still refused to play the show to that extent. They'd sold this event by saying it was to spend time with the bachelorettes. Spending time with her didn't include her body.

Besides, Roth was going to bid on her. Enticing other bidders would defeat the purpose of her securing his promise. Autumn had tuned out Mrs. Stephens' listing of her accomplishments and accolades, only paying attention when she opened the bidding.

"Now, ladies and gentlemen. We'll start the bidding at ten."

Immediately, the hand Autumn didn't want to see shot up. She had to give it to Cartwright, his reflexes were still sharp. Autumn's attempt not to frantically search for Roth wasn't a complete failure, but she couldn't categorize it as a success either.

"We have ten from Mr. Cartwright, do I hear eleven?"

It was well established that any number mentioned had an unspoken thousand behind it. So, Mrs. Stephens didn't do something as uncouth as speaking the entire amount.

"Eleven."

Without her consent, Autumn's head swung to her left. The voice didn't belong to Roth. Who the hell was that guy? And what the hell was taking Roth so long to weigh in? While she tried not to freak out, the unknown man and Mr. Cartwright entered a bidding war. Autumn was very nearly losing hope when the deep, gruff voice she'd been waiting for entered the fray.

"One hundred."

A collective gasp swept through the crowd and all heads turned toward Roth. Striding up the aisle as if he were strolling through a field of high grass, he approached the stage.

"Well!" Mrs. Stephens sounded flustered and momentarily forgot her role as auctioneer. It was completely understandable as the mystery man and Cartwright were inching their way toward thirty thousand before Roth interrupted with his bid. Clearing her throat, his mother collected herself to continue.

"We have a bid for one hundred. Do I hear any others?" After a brief pause, she repeated the question two more times.

"Going once, twice. The winning bid goes to Rothschild Stephens. Thank you, Mr. Stephens for your generous contribution. Please come and collect your beautiful date."

Autumn was positive the smile she'd glued onto her face looked as phony as it felt. She had to call upon all the years of training from her mother and the skills she'd perfected practicing law to keep from showing the depth of her emotions at the moment. When she'd asked Roth to bid on her, she hadn't meant for him to shell out enough money to fund a program for a year. *What the hell was he thinking?*

Even before his mother had proclaimed his bid as the winner, he was already approaching the stage. When he reached the edge, Autumn lost the ability to look anywhere but at him. Once he extended his hand, she didn't have to tell her feet to move. They took her to him.

The callouses on his palm felt rough against hers, but she liked it. The warmth of his grasp travelled up her arm before radiating to the rest of her body.

"Let's go, Sugar."

Roth's touch was already wreaking havoc. Then, the man had to go and open his mouth. *Why didn't he just stay quiet?* Autumn's new focus became concentrating on not melting into a puddle before she made it to the bottom of the stage and away from the prying eyes of the people in the room.

With her hand completely engulfed in his, Autumn studiously avoided eye contact with everyone until she and Roth came to a stop in front of a long rectangular table. Seated behind it were two women with laptops. Only when one of them spoke, did Autumn dare to focus on anything else.

"Hey there, Roth. Autumn."

"Ellen Sue." Roth and Autumn spoke in unison, acknowledging the woman who was unashamedly Lone Star Ridge's most prolific gossip.

"Is this where I pay my pledge?"

"It sure is. You can settle up with me or Charity Ann. We're both set up to take cash, check, or mobile transfer."

Charity's face flushed, but she neither confirmed nor denied Ellen Sue's statement. The way she ducked her head and stared at the computer screen told Autumn the crush she'd had on Roth was still very much alive.

Autumn didn't blame her. Growing up, there were very few girls who didn't have a crush on at least one of the Stephens boys. Sometimes it was all three. They were all tall and thickly built with dark hair. The only major difference between them was their eye color. Ryker's was the same azure blue of their mother's, while Roth had his father's honey-colored eyes and Rhinehart was an interesting mixture of the two.

"I'll do the electronic transfer."

Autumn fought off the sensation of abandonment when Roth released her hand to pull out his cellphone.

"Right on here is the QR code and other stuff we've set up to make things easier for y'all."

Ellen Sue moved a small pop-up banner closer to Roth showing him the information he'd need to complete the electronic transfer of funds.

Autumn wasn't trying to snoop, but his nearness and the way he held the phone made it impossible for her to miss him casually following the prompts on the screen to complete his donation. Not having access to her trust fund yet, meant she'd have to move a little something from an investment account to drop that kind of money on anything.

Leave it to her maternal grandfather to make the archaic stipulation that she could only access the trust before the age of forty, if she got married. Thinking of her trust took her mind to her close call with marrying the philandering Russell. Even after she called things off, she ended up having to block him on everything to get him to go away.

After seeing his face in a few pictures on social media, she didn't dare tell Nick about his attempts to contact her. Although he and Roth had returned to their post, she didn't doubt one of them had the connections to reach out and touch Russell from thousands of miles away.

"Okay! It looks like you're all set!"

Ellen Sue's chipper delivery almost matched the glee on her face. Her gaze pinged between the two of them lingering on their hands. Once he'd completed the transaction, Roth had recaptured her hand, folding it into his larger one. When Ellen Sue looked up at her face again, Autumn couldn't resist lifting a single questioning eyebrow.

She already knew Ellen Sue was going to jump into her favorite town group chat and start the rumors. Because, even though Roth and Nick had been the best of friends since childhood, Autumn and Roth had never been hand-holding close. He watched over her as fiercely as Nick and was likely part of the reason the boys her age were afraid to ask her out until her senior year of high school.

Because who wanted to date the girl who had two extra-large, overzealous body guards hovering? By the time they accepted their commissions in the army, she was almost ready for college and could keep the undesirables away without them standing behind her mean-mugging any male within a thirty-foot radius.

With a curt goodbye and head tilt to the two women,

Roth gave Autumn a gentle tug, getting her feet moving. After a few steps, she realized they were heading toward the exit.

"Roth, I can't just leave."

Slowing to a stop, Roth peered down at her.

"Why not? I told you I was planning to go before the bidding started. I only stayed as long as I did because you asked me to help you. I helped. I'm done here. I figured you wouldn't want to stay here for any of the questions."

Autumn glanced around to be certain no one was in earshot before speaking.

"I don't want to stay for questions, but I have one of my own. Why in the world would you bid that kind of money on me?"

One muscular shoulder lifted and lowered, causing his tuxedo to stretch and relax to contain the bulge.

"I wasn't about to spend another ten minutes countering those two with pennies. So, I bid high enough to shut 'em up."

"Okay, but—" Autumn looked around again and lowered her voice. "But, 100K? Seriously, Roth? That's excessive."

"Says you." Roth released a heaving sigh as he looked at the doorway a scant twenty feet away.

"Look, are you staying or leaving with me? I have about three more minutes left in me before I start biting people's heads off. Since I promised my mama I wouldn't embarrass her, I need to hightail it."

"Well, I—" Autumn's reply was cut off by an excited Virginia Stephens.

"There you two are!"

Roth's groan was audible and his thick beard wasn't any help camouflaging his grimace.

"Hey, Mama. Aren't you shirking your duties? Weren't you just on stage?"

Roth's questions couldn't have been more transparent.

Autumn ducked her head to avoid laughing aloud. Mrs. Stephens brushed him off with a light swat to his shoulder.

"You don't worry about me and my duties. The ladies and I have a system. I stopped at the table and Ellen Sue said you'd already come by to make good on your bid."

The smile on her face reached her eyes, making them sparkle with delight.

"I'm certain your bid will be the highest of the night. Did you two plan this?" Mrs. Stephens looked between them. "I know it took some arm twisting for me to get this one here, and when I talked to Carla, she said it wasn't much easier wrangling you, Missy."

Autumn shook her head. "Ma'am, I can honestly say I had no intention of Roth bidding such a large amount of money on me."

It was then that Mrs. Stephen's gaze darted to their joined hands. Her smile went to megawatt levels.

"Oh... Oh! Well, okay then. I just wanted to thank you both for being such good sports and being so generous." Reaching up, she cupped the side of Roth's face, delivering two gentle taps before dropping her hand. "I'm so proud of you."

She seemed to not expect a response from him because she immediately turned her attention to Autumn. "I won't hold you kids up any longer. I can tell my son is chomping at the bit to get out of here. You two have a great evening. Autumn, I'll let your parents know Roth is seeing you home."

With her declaration, she walked away. She hadn't made it more than a step before Roth was on the move again, pulling Autumn behind him. After a close call with her heel in a crack on the sidewalk outside the building, she jerked on his hand. Hard.

"Roth!"

Stopping immediately, he looked at her. There was a strange look in his eyes before he wiped it away.

"What's wrong?"

"Your legs are much longer than mine, and I'm wearing six-inch heels. That's what's wrong."

"Do you need me to carry you?"

As glorious as his suggestion sounded, Autumn shook her head. "No. I just need you to slow down. And where are we going? We passed the valet stand."

"I didn't valet. I parked myself."

Chapter Five

Roth's gaze raked over Autumn's form, partially inspecting her condition to see if he needed to follow through with his suggestion to carry her. Even knowing Nick would likely have something to say if he were to walk outside and see his sister in Roth's arms didn't stop Roth from considering it.

He saw the question building in her eyes, wondering why he hadn't simply used the valet services. His reason was a longer discussion he'd rather not have. It wasn't just about him maintaining control over his own vehicle. But, he'd prefer if he didn't have to discuss it.

"I don't understand, Roth. You didn't valet?"

"I don't know how to say it any plainer, Sugar. I didn't hand my keys over to a stranger. I parked in the lot over there and walked to the door in less time than it would've taken me to wait in the line for them to get to me."

"Strangers? Roth, those kids are local. I recognized more than a couple of them. There's no way they aren't familiar to you."

"Doesn't matter if they look familiar. *I* don't know them." Releasing a huffing breath, he held his arms slightly away from his body with his palms facing Autumn. "Now... Back to my original question. Do you need me to carry you, or can you manage in those things?"

Looking pointedly from her shoes to her face, Roth waited a beat for her to respond. When she simply tilted her head to one side, he made an executive decision. His desire to get away from the event overruled his good sense. Closing the distance between them, he had her swung up in his arms bridal style before she could form her response.

"Roth!" Her exclamation was a cross between a gasping protest and a scandalized squeak.

"What? You were takin' too long. Besides, those sky-high skinny heels have gotta be hell on your feet."

Long strides took them farther away from the community center and closer to his truck. He might've fudged a little when he indicated where he'd parked. Because parking was blocked off for valet use, he'd actually left his Dually in the lot behind the one used by the event. So, if he hadn't scooped her into his arms, she would've cursed him out once she realized how far away it was.

Roth allowed his gaze to travel over their surroundings protectively while patently refusing to look at her. He was certain Autumn was staring at him, because he felt the weight of it boring into him.

"My legs work perfectly fine, Rothschild Stephens. And, my shoes are actually very comfortable. A quality shoe in the correct size doesn't cause foot pain."

Biting back his automatic response about how perfectly fine her legs were, Roth focused on her statement regarding her shoes.

"You sound like Ryker when he talks about spending money on a good pair of boots."

"You should listen to us. Your brother knows boots, and I know women's shoes."

Grunting as a form of reply, Roth didn't contradict her assertion. He was too busy trying to talk his cock out of plumping in his pants once her soft fingertips brushed the back of his neck when she draped her arms around his shoulders to hold on. The action made him wish he'd gotten out of the habit of cutting his hair so short, instead of letting it grow.

Roth's predicament was the torture of his own making. He could've very well asked her to stay at the doorway while he went to get his truck. But, he didn't like the idea of her waiting outside at night. Despite the valets and others being around, he didn't think it was the safest option.

However, holding her in his arms was a slice of heaven wrapped in hell. Because, having Autumn's plush curves molding to his body was exquisite. Heavenly. Knowing he probably wouldn't and shouldn't act on anything his cock suggested was the hell. And it was excruciating.

When he finally stopped beside his dual cab pickup truck, he was reluctant to set Autumn back on her feet. A soft breeze brushed across his neck as she spoke.

"Roth?"

"Hm?"

"Why did you stop?"

"Because this is my truck."

"Oh." Silence reigned between them for a few moments before she spoke again. "Are you gonna put me down?"

No. I don't want to. The words flashed across his mind, but he didn't utter them aloud. His grip tightened reflexively before he forced himself to bend his knees and lower her heeled feet to the asphalt.

The thanks she murmured was soft, but Roth didn't miss the hitch in her voice. Finally, he was unable to stop himself from looking at her face again. Her beautiful, brown eyes were so dark they appeared bottomless. Her full lips seemed to form a slight pout, but it could've been his imagination.

It took him a solid minute to remember himself and unlock the door. When her hand landed on the handle, Roth was unable to contain the grumbling growl. Autumn snatched her fingers back as her gaze snapped to his.

"Did you just growl at me?"

"I don't know what you're talking about, but why was your hand on that door? You know better."

Before she could gear up to give him shit about it, he opened the door and held out his hand.

"Come on, Sugar. I'll help you in."

Although he'd braced himself to withstand having her soft hand in his again, he still nearly closed his eyes after she accepted his assistance. Brushing past him lightly, she held onto him as she stepped onto the running board before climbing into the truck.

It wasn't strictly necessary, but he transferred his hold to her back and thigh to help her slide onto the seat. Mistake. A big one. Not monumental, but a mistake nonetheless. His only consolation was that her soft inhale told him he wasn't the only one to feel it.

"Thank you." Leaning away, Autumn's gratitude was spoken so softly he would've missed if he weren't so close.

As if it was a well-practiced routine, Roth tugged at the safety belt, stretching it across her torso, clicking it into the buckle. As he pulled away, he couldn't stop himself from inhaling her tempting scent. Capturing the aroma, he stepped back, closing the door. As he rounded the front of the truck, his phone buzzed in his pocket.

He had one hand on the driver's side door and the other held the phone when he looked at the incoming call. *Shit.* It was Nick. Heaving a sigh, he answered as he continued to get into the vehicle.

"Yeah."

"Don't yeah me." Nick's voice was a barely audible

strained whisper. Roth frowned as he tried to hear what his friend was saying.

"How the fuck did you let Autumn talk you into dropping 100K? Never mind. I don't want to know. But why did y'all skip out and leave me by myself?"

Ignoring Nick's question, Roth asked one of his own. "Why are you whispering?"

"Because...Since y'all skipped out and left me, I'm in the bathroom hiding from my own damn mama. She's being extra pushy with the introducing me to single women and hinting around that I should bid on someone. And I don't have a shield, because y'all *Fucking. Left. Me.*"

He really shouldn't have, but Roth couldn't hold back his laughter at Nick's distress. Pressing the button to start the engine, he waited a beat for the call to automatically connect before he spoke again. Glancing at Autumn, he caught the confusion in her expression.

"Number one, we didn't leave you. How were we supposed to know you wanted to cut out? You left us first, remember?"

"Stop bringing up old stuff and—Hold on."

Autumn clamped her hand over her mouth in an attempt to stem her giggles when they heard Nick apparently responding to his mother knocking on the bathroom door.

"Yes, ma'am. I'll be right out. I just need to wash my hands." His voice was low again when he hissed, "See! She's standing outside the door like I'm four-years-old instead of forty-one. I'm gonna get both of y'all for this."

He paused briefly when Autumn couldn't contain her laughter. The rich sound of her glee filled the cabin of Roth's truck. Instead of joining in, Roth simply stared at her. She was even more beautiful when she laughed.

"You know what?" Nick started up again. "Since y'all think this is funny, I'm gonna tell mama y'all snuck off together. She'll be blowing up your phone first thing in the morning trying to get details, Tum."

When Roth chuffed at his threat, Nick added, "Oh, don't think you're getting off the hook Mr-I-don't-leave-my-ranch. You'll be getting more frequent dinner invitations. As a matter of fact, I'm gonna tell your mama too."

Roth's gaze shot to Autumn's. Her laughter had dried up and she returned his stare. One corner of her bottom lip was caught between her teeth.

"You're too late. My mama already knows we left together. She volunteered to let your parents know I'm escorting Autumn home, to keep them from worrying. So, you'll have to come up with a better plan."

"You know what?" Nick huffed. However, he didn't add to his sentence or answer his own question. Instead, he ended the call.

Breaking away from Autumn's expressive eyes, Roth secured his own safety belt, put the truck into gear and navigated the vehicle out of the parking lot. Once Nick ended the call, the system automatically switched to the radio.

The distinct sound of Zane Rivers' voice came from the speakers as he sang about missing out on love. The song was a slight departure from Tremor's normal stuff, but something about the words caught Roth's attention. Primarily keeping his focus on the road, he shot a quick glance at Autumn when she began humming along to the melody.

"I can turn it up, if you like." The offer popped out without Roth's mouth consulting with his brain.

"Are you saying you don't want to hear my off-key humming?"

A smile tugged at the corner of his lips at the false insult he detected in her tone.

"Sugar, I don't care if your voice is so bad it would crack

glass. I just thought you liked the song and might want me to turn it up for you."

"Mhm."

Roth's grin grew after he saw the cute little twist of her lips when she responded, knowing she was pretending to be offended by his cracked glass comment. One thing which appeared to still be true about Autumn was that she loved music. While she was good at many things, singing wasn't one of them. But, he didn't want her to feel like she couldn't enjoy a song or sing aloud whenever she wanted.

Taking a left turn onto the sparsely lit four lane road leading toward his ranch, Roth hazarded another glance at Autumn. Her arms were folded across her middle while she looked out the window. Reaching over, he tugged on her left arm until she unfolded both. His fingers glided from her elbow to her wrist before he folded her hand into his.

"Hey. I didn't mean to make you self-conscious. You didn't have to stop singing."

"You didn't. The song is over."

He'd been so focused on her, he hadn't really noticed the music shifting to a different band.

"Huh. I guess you're right."

They rode in silence for a little while, but Roth didn't feel any pressure to fill it. Autumn seemed to be of the same mind as she didn't initiate any conversation. It wasn't until he was nearing the turn off to the Lazy Creek did she speak up.

"Roth?"

He glanced at her in response.

"Where are you taking me?"

Until she'd asked, he'd been on auto-pilot. He'd even started to slow down in preparation for turning onto the private road leading to his ranch.

"Shit, Sugar. I forgot to ask where you were staying while you're here."

Humor coated her words. "So, I take that to mean you were taking me home with you?"

She was laughing, but her question sent a jolt straight to his cock. Gritting his teeth and redirecting his thoughts, Roth tried to shake it off.

"I was definitely heading to my place."

"Just because you dropped six figures doesn't mean you can get handsy with me, Rothschild Stephens."

Roth tilted his head slightly, wondering if he was hearing what he thought he heard. *Was Autumn flirting with him?* He'd never be able to explain why he did and said what he did next.

"Are you sure about that, Sugar?"

Her hand was still engulfed by his, so he tangled their fingers together. Then, using his thumb, he traced an abstract design on her thigh. While her dress was a barrier between the blunt tip of his digit and her soft skin, it wasn't a deterrent.

Releasing a soft gasp, Autumn's fingers gripped his, but she didn't attempt to move his hand away from her leg.

Chapter Six

This isn't real. It's a dream. None of this is happening. Those three sentences were on a loop in Autumn's head as she tried to maintain her composure. There was no way Roth Stephens was flirting with her. Him holding her hand the majority of the ride already had her senses on high alert. The feelings multiplied exponentially when he uttered his question in that deep, gruff voice of his.

Since she'd moved to the Las Vegas area, she didn't often encounter anyone with his distinctive Texas drawl. Even when she did meet someone with hints of Texas in their voice, it didn't have nearly the same effect as hearing him call her Sugar and asking her whatever the hell it was he said afterwards.

"What's the matter, Sugar? Cat got your tongue?"

Digging deep, Autumn finally gathered herself enough to reply. "Are you saying you *do* expect compensation for your generous donation to the Ladies' Auxiliary?"

The sudden swerve made Autumn grasp the "Oh Shit" handle to keep herself steady. Just in front of them, the headlights shined across the gravel road leading to the gate with the

Lazy Creek sign above it. If he hadn't stopped the truck, they would've arrived at his ranch house in less than ten minutes.

His hold on her hand tightened, and his voice dropped an octave. The heat in his honey-colored eyes made her gulp in an attempt to swallow her ill-advised accusation.

"Autumn. I don't give a shit how this all started. I didn't *buy* you. Nor your time. Look me in my eyes and tell me you think I'm expecting you to put out because I gave money to a charity on your behalf?"

Autumn winced when he said her name. In less than two hours she'd gone from Tummy to Sugar to Autumn. And as much as she didn't like him calling her Tummy, she liked him using Autumn even less. Sugar was now her favorite, and she wanted nothing else coming from his lips when referring to her. Autumn figured her lipstick was likely a mess after the hell she was giving her bottom lip.

"No, Roth. I don't think you expect sex from me because you donated money."

His nod was curt. Autumn was unable to move when the distance between them shrank to inches.

"Do you also understand that what does or does not happen between us, whatever it is, will be a mutual act?"

Autumn's pulse thundered in her ears. *Was he asking what it sounded like he was asking? No. That's not possible.* Never. Not once in the more than twenty-five years she'd known him had Roth hinted at seeing her as anyone other than Nick's little sister. Not even when her feminine attributes announced themselves loudly in her teens and many of the male gender began giving her attention did he indicate any interest. He was protective of her, but it was simply a byproduct of him and Nick being best friends and Roth not having a younger sister of his own.

"Sugar."

Roth's molasses dipped voice pulled her from her internal

thoughts. Relocating her gaze from his lips to his eyes, she waited for him to continue.

"If you're uncomfortable with any of this, you just say the word. I'm gonna take you wherever you want to go regardless. I just wanted to clear the air."

The intensity of his gaze combined with his nearness was enough to addle Autumn's thoughts completely. Yet, somehow she managed to make complete sentences.

"I'm... Um... I'm staying with Grandma Daley at the Sunset."

Roth's stare had dropped to her mouth with her first word. But he looked back into her eyes when she mentioned her grandparent's ranch, which was adjacent to his. A creek served as a natural barrier between the two properties.

"Okay. That's where I'll take you."

When his grip on her fingers loosened, and he shifted to move away, Autumn surprised both of them by grabbing his lapel with her free hand.

"I didn't say I was ready to go there. I was just letting you know."

The space between them shrank down to millimeters. With his nose almost touching hers, Autumn could make out the variations in his eye color in the dim lighting of the truck's interior.

"What are you trying to say, Sugar?"

What was she trying to say? Instead of answering either of them, Autumn tossed caution into the wind and closed the remaining distance separating him. The wiry hairs of his mustache and beard lightly abraded her skin, but his lips were inviting.

She may have initiated their kiss, but Roth quickly took over. Delving into her mouth, his tongue danced with hers, setting off a fluttering in her belly which quickly traveled to the apex of her thighs. Her hair, carefully arranged to waterfall over one shoulder, was going to be well and truly mussed from his fingers invading her curls, tugging with the perfect amount of force.

Autumn couldn't care less. He could loosen every pin she used to achieve the style and scatter them to the wind so long as he didn't stop kissing and touching her. The sound of the seat belt releasing was almost as loud as her breathing when he let go of her fingers to unsnap the buckle.

A hitching moan issued from Autumn when his dexterous digits skimmed the outline of her breast before covering the globe. The barrier of her dress and bra were inconsequential as he zeroed in on her puckered nipple, giving it a pinch.

"Mmm! Roth!" Her gasp was met with a growl as he kissed his way down to the crook of her neck where he latched on to the sensitive skin.

"You smell fucking delicious."

Using the hand in her hair, he tilted her head back to gain better access. The bodice of her dress was shifted to the side. His new quest was obvious. Raining kisses along her collarbone, he'd just reached the top of her breast when bright lights nearly blinded Autumn. Her eyes closed tighter against the intrusion that was like a dousing of cold water.

Although the vehicle passed them by, the invasion had snapped them both out of their lust filled fog enough to realize they were parked on the side of the road making out like horny teenagers instead of full-grown adults.

"Fuck, Sugar. I'm sorry. I got a little carried away."

Roth's forehead rested against hers. Gently moving it side to side, he placed one lingering kiss on her lips before releasing her. Stroking his beard, Autumn couldn't resist running her thumb along his lips before dropping her hands into her lap.

"Don't be sorry. I'm not."

One large hand covered both of hers, squeezing before he released them. Reaching across her again, he re-buckled her seat belt. When he was done, he drummed his fingers along the top of the gearshift.

"You deserve better than to be felt up on the side of the road."

Autumn watched him for a moment. Laying her hand on his, she halted the tapping.

"You're acting like you jumped me without my permission. *I kissed you*, Roth."

"Yeah, but you weren't about to strip me naked before that car drove by."

"Who says?" She was wearing a flirty smirk when he whipped his head around to look at her.

"Oh. I see you want that juicy ass spanked."

Autumn wasn't sure how she flipped Roth's switch. But, she had no regrets. Not with the way her core clenched when he promised to spank her ass. Her lady bits' only response to his threat was, 'yes please.'

Without another word, he put the truck into gear and completed the turn onto Lazy Creek Road. The drive, which should've taken ten minutes, was greatly reduced. Sooner than she expected, they rolled to a stop in the attached garage and Roth was rounding the truck flinging open her door.

She barely had her safety belt unbuckled before he turned her in the seat bracing his hands on her knees. Her gasp was swallowed by his mouth while he pressed her knees open wide enough to accommodate his hips. This kiss was different from the first. The intensity ratcheted up astronomically when she felt his hard body pressed against her softness.

Autumn couldn't be bothered by the slight ripping sound as her legs widened beyond the limits of the split in her dress. She was too caught up in the feel of Roth's big hands roaming her body. Heat bloomed from her center making her wind her hips, seeking relief.

One second, there was buttery soft leather beneath her

bottom, the next Roth's calloused hands were cradling her ass, pressing her panty clad pussy against his belt buckle. The completely decorative accessory hit her folds at precisely the right angle when he lifted her from the seat.

The trip through the lower floor of the house was accomplished amid kisses, touches and the removal of garments. By the time they reached his bedroom, Autumn was clad only in her bra and bottoms. There was no room for embarrassment over the short tights designed to keep her inner thighs from being rubbed raw when she wore dresses. The way Roth devoured her with his gaze, she may as well have been wearing skimpy lingerie.

He'd tossed the duvet back and placed her on the bed. She lay semi reclined as he shucked off the rest his clothing. The way his shaft tented his boxer briefs clearly indicated his arousal. Her fingers traveled the waist band of her underwear only to be grasped by his.

"Uh-uh. That's my job. You just stay right there and wait for me to take care of you."

Standing back upright, he stuck his thumbs into the waist band of his underwear sliding them off along with his pants. When he straightened up, Autumn nearly swallowed her tongue. *Ho-ly shit.*

It was one thing to believe a man was generously endowed. It was totally different to see that, not only did he receive more than his fair share of penis, he had the double blessing of length *and* girth. She didn't even realize she'd closed her legs until his hands appeared on her knees pressing them apart again. Hovering above her, Roth wore a cocky smirk.

"You wouldn't be havin' second thoughts would you, Sugar?"

Autumn's vocal cords weren't responding to commands, but she managed to shake her head. Even if she had to soak in Epsom salts for hours, she wasn't backing out. Snaking her hand between them, she wrapped her fingers as far as they could reach around his thickness, stroking his length. *Damn!* She was definitely gonna be sore tomorrow.

"Fuck..." Dragging the word out in a groan, Roth tugged his hips away her questing digits while dropping lower to capture her lips. "Not yet, Sugar. We don't want this over before it starts."

Keeping her occupied with drugging kisses, he rid her of her undergarments. Autumn was nearly out of her mind with need by the time he lay on his belly, with her legs thrown over his shoulders and his head between her thighs. His first swipe at her folds had her back bowing.

"Damn, Sugar. You taste even better than you smell, and you smell fucking delicious."

That was the last thing Roth said before he coaxed her pearl from its hood and proceeded to suck her soul from her body via her sensitive clit.

Chapter Seven

Even if he'd wanted to, Roth couldn't contain the satisfied groan issuing from his chest once the first trickle of Autumn's essence landed on his tongue. She really did taste better than he envisioned from her scent. He could see himself quickly becoming addicted to her flavor.

Only his broad shoulders kept her from smothering him with her thick thighs when her body stiffened, and she released a keening wail. The trickle of her feminine juice became a flood that Roth greedily lapped up. Barely pausing to breathe, he dipped his tongue into her channel to capture every drop of his new favorite snack.

"Roth!"

His name was a raspy gasp snatched from her throat, giving Roth more incentive to do whatever he could to draw more of her vocal appreciation. Pulling back from her mound with a parting kiss, he replaced his tongue with two fingers. Slipping them inside her velvet walls, he curled them in a come-hither motion, seeking the internal bundle of nerves designed to send her over the edge into another orgasm. He wanted an additional blessing of her sweetness before he gave into the demands of his cock.

Incoherent babble fell from Autumn's lips, bringing a cocky smirk to Roth's face.

"What's that, Sugar? I didn't quite understand you."

He didn't let up enough for her to gather herself to think clearly to form an answer. No. Instead, he remained where he was at the apex of her legs manipulating her secret place, allowing the air from his breath to blow across her sensitive mons.

"Oh...fuck...Roth!..."

"Was that a request?" Unable to resist, Roth gave her clit a suckling kiss before releasing it with a pop. "Answer me, Sugar. Are you sayin' you want me to fuck you?"

As he teased her, Roth had to pull his own hips back from the bed since his cock had hardened to the point of painful stiffness. Pre-cum leaked from the tip, dripping onto the sheets. He probably wouldn't be able to keep himself from sliding into her slick heat for much longer—whether she responded to his taunting or not.

More disjointed mumbles came from Autumn amidst her twisting and squirming on the bed. Clamping an arm around one lush thigh, he held her in place.

"Where do you think you're going? I'm not nearly done with you."

Rising to his knees, he kept ahold of her leg, anchoring it to his chest as he rose. Once her ass rested on his thighs, he allowed his gaze to travel from her delicious pussy, up over her heavy breasts to her lust fogged eyes. Roth brought the fingers which had previously delved inside her honeyed walls to his mouth, licking her sweet cream from his digits. After he was satisfied he'd captured it all, he wrapped his hand around his length, tapping the head against her slick center.

"Now... Use your words, Sugar. Tell me what you want."

Autumn's pretty face twisted in what appeared to be lust and frustration. Her teeth gave her bottom lip hell as a guttural moan tore from her throat. A single word finally pushed past her lips.

"Please..."

"Please, what?" Roth aimed his cock at the opening to paradise, swirling it in her essence, but not entering to put them both out of their misery. "Talk to me, Sugar. You beg real pretty, but you haven't told me what you want me to do for you."

Roth nearly folded when he saw the shiny wetness gather in her eyes. If she hadn't finally gained the ability to form words again, he would definitely have proceeded without them.

"Please fuck me, Roth. I need to feel you." Released in a raspy, gritty huff, Autumn's declaration had barely hit the air before Roth sheathed himself inside her heated core.

"Fuuuck...Sugar..."

With his arms wrapped around her thighs, Roth fed his length into Autumn's channel inch by excruciating decadent inch. *How was it possible for her pussy to feel so good wrapped around his cock? And why had he waited so long to experience it?*

Neither question was voiced aloud and both were quickly pushed to the back of his mind as he bottomed out with his balls resting in the valley between her delicious pussy and her ass. Withdrawing from her heat, he tilted his pelvis as he stroked back inside.

Roth knew he was already addicted to the taste of her sweetness; now he had to contend with the possibility of being obsessed with sinking into the heaven on earth located between her plush thighs. A light sheen of sweat covered his chest and arms and beaded on his brow. His eyes pinged between watching the sensual play of emotions across her face to her breasts bouncing with each stroke, to the place where they were joined together.

His lightly tanned cock delving between the brown lips of her labia to enter her pink center was a fascinatingly erotic visual, compelling him to stare. Roth couldn't say which was better, watching it or feeling it. When Autumn tilted her hips, feeding her pussy into his strokes, his eyes slammed shut, leaving him only to feel.

Gritting his teeth, he fought against the sensation building inside him, urging him to let go. To paint her walls with his release. The sharp bite of pain to his forearms lifted his eyelids to see her gripping him with her short, blunt nails digging into his skin. Using her hold as leverage she fucked herself on and off his length making it nearly impossible for him not to come.

"What do you think you're doing, Sugar?" Roth didn't recognize the deep, gruff voice as his own, but it didn't deter him. "Do you think you can just fuck me and take what you want? Hm?"

Releasing her thighs one by one, he twisted his arms breaking her hold. Ignoring her mewls of protest, he pulled out of her slick heat. Before she could work up too much of a fuss, he flipped her onto her belly and pulled her onto her knees. The satisfying crack of his open palm meeting the silky skin of her ass drew another cocky smile to his lips.

Autumn's gasp was in contrast to the wiggling undulation of her hips, moving toward him seeking the contact again.

"You like that, huh? I didn't forget I owed that ass a spanking, but you're working on more."

Lining himself up, he sank back inside her heated channel. The grimace on his face belied the pure pleasure he felt. He wouldn't last much longer. Delivering another smack to her rounded cheeks, he took care with the placement of his hand and the force he used. Pleasure, not pain was his goal. The responding convulsions of her walls around his length was all the confirmation he needed.

The volume of Autumn's moans increased, reaching a crescendo when her internal muscles clamped around his shaft, making his efforts to hold off his own orgasm fruitless. The way her pussy fluttered around his cock practically sucked the cum from his balls.

Falling onto his extended arms, his chest rested lightly against her back and he instinctively nuzzled the side of her neck. Growling grunts were all he could manage as he gave up the fight and succumbed to the siren call of her delicious core milking him for everything he had.

"Fuck, Sugar."

Breathing heavily, it took Roth several minutes to gather himself enough to separate from Autumn. The moment he did, she toppled over onto her side, curling her knees to her chest. Without thought, he wrapped his arms around her, pulling her into him, with her beautiful ass tucked against his groin. His spent cock had the audacity to twitch at the contact —despite him not being in the position to make good on anything the greedy monster wanted to do, for at least ten...no fifteen minutes.

Once they were both breathing evenly, Roth let Autumn go and rolled off the bed. Tugging the cover over her to ward off the chill, he went to the ensuite bathroom, returning with a warm towel. Sitting next to her on the bed, he took a second to simply observe her. Her perfectly styled hair was now a combination of mussed and smashed curls.

Her disheveled appearance inspired a modicum of pride in being responsible for her current well-fucked state. She was essentially boneless when he nudged her shoulder rolling her onto her back. Parting her legs, he went about gently cleaning the mess he'd made of her.

A moan preceded the capture of his hand between her

legs, and Roth's gaze transferred from inspecting her pretty pussy to looking into her beautiful face. Both of her hands were on his arm with her blunt nails lightly digging into his skin again.

"What's wrong, Sugar?"

Squirming, Autumn regarded him beneath half lowered eyelids. Her lips pursed into a pout so alluring he had to kiss them. Soft beneath his, they opened allowing him to delve his tongue inside. Flexing his fingers brought forth another squirming moan.

Pulling back slightly, Roth searched Autumn's face.

"Talk to me, Sugar. I can't fix it, if you don't tell me what it is."

Another flex of his cloth covered finger elicited a pelvic tilt and tighter clamp of her hold on his arm.

"Too sensitive..."

A sliver of pink appeared when she swiped her tongue across her lips before pulling it back into her mouth. Roth greedily followed the motion.

"What's too sensitive, baby? This?" The slightest flick of his finger against her clit drew a hissing inhale from her.

"Roth...!" His name was a moan and a plea on her lips.

Leaning closer, he placed pecking kisses on her plump lips. "Want me to stop, Sugar? I can. If that's what you want."

The tilting of her hips and transfer of her hold from her forearm to his shoulders, pulling him closer, was in contrast to the protesting moans she released. But, Roth wouldn't relent to her actions alone. He needed the words. He craved them. So, he demanded them of her before moving further.

"Don't. Don't stop. More. Please. Give me more."

Roth happily complied. Swooping down, he placed hungry kisses on her lips. Then, trailing down her neck and over her collarbone, he latched onto one turgid peak, showering it with attention. The towel had been tossed aside as he coaxed her clit from its hood; her slickness coating his fingers to facilitate his activities.

After lavishing the same attention on her other breast, he kissed his way down her body until he was once again face-to-pussy. Kissing her folds reverently, he looked up to see Autumn watching him. In a move which inspired a squealing shriek to spring from her lips, he rolled onto his back, positioning her fragrant center above his face.

"Moisturize my beard, Sugar."

Chapter Eight

"If you keep wiggling your ass against me, I'm gonna have you instead of my morning oats for breakfast."

Roth's gruff voice in her ear sent a sensual tingle straight to Autumn's core. One would think after the night she'd had letting him put that monster of a dick inside her as often as it got hard, she would've immediately stilled her squirming. Instead, her bratty side made an appearance, writing a check her pussy would have to cash.

She couldn't hold back the pout when instead of the prize she wanted, she received a light stinging tap to her backside. Testing Roth's gangster, Autumn tilted her hips as if to offer her ass for another smack. His long, thick fingers clamped onto her side locking her into position. Autumn wasn't able to prevent the giggle and shimmy when Roth's beard tickled her neck and shoulder when he growled into her ear again.

"Sugar... You seem bound and determined to test me."

Autumn's giggles cut off sharply when she was suddenly relocated to her back with the hulking cowboy leaning over her, braced on his thick arms. In the dim light filtering in through the curtains, his expression seemed fierce, but full of promises. Instead of fear, Autumn felt her core slickening in anticipation. One corner of her mouth tipped up and a single eyebrow lifted in a universal look of challenge.

Responding to her nonverbal defiance, Roth returned her half grin with a smirk of his own.

"So, that's what you're up to, huh? You want me to have that pussy for breakfast."

Leaning down, he captured her lips in a kiss which quickly transitioned into him keeping his promise of having her for his first meal of the day. Following her second leg shaking orgasm, Autumn tapped out. Brushing her hair from her face, she gasped for air as Roth flopped onto the bed beside her. She was definitely gonna need to soak in some good bath salts, but it was totally worth it. Even though she wasn't thinking about moving, one beefy arm reached out keeping her close to his side.

Their heads were inches apart on the same pillow. Autumn couldn't stop herself from studying Roth as he lay there with his eyes closed. He looked so relaxed. Free. Far different from the expression he wore when she first saw him last night. For that matter, it was different from the rare photos she'd seen of him following his time in the military.

She never did learn why he'd taken an early retirement or why he'd spent almost two years in Ironhaven, South Dakota. Nick said Roth was working on a ranch there, which was additionally confusing because his grandpa had a fully functioning ranch he could've worked on. Roth didn't return until his grandfather became sick and was no longer able to run the ranch by himself.

When he passed away, Roth took over completely. Autumn wasn't sure how much input his brothers had. Nick had made it seem like the other two Stephens boys didn't have the desire to be in the ranching business. Of course, she couldn't ask too many questions of her brother. If she did, he'd start to wonder why she was so interested in Roth and what was going on in his life.

The distant sound of buzzing interrupted the quiet of the room, ruining Roth's peaceful expression by putting a frown on his face.

"Fuck... Who the fuck is calling at the butt crack of dawn?"

Roth grumbled, but made no moves to actually locate the buzzing interloper to find the answer. However, his mention of the time had Autumn bolting upright in the bed. For completely illogical reasons that made perfect sense to her suddenly frantic mind, she scrambled to grab the sheet, pulling it up to hide her nakedness.

It was only when she popped up that Roth put any serious effort into appearing more alert.

"What's wrong, Sugar?"

"It's morning."

Autumn's succinct response seemed pretty explanatory to her, but Roth simply stared at her. Clutching the sheet harder, she ignored the way his frown deepened when he saw she'd covered herself up.

"It's morning, Roth! I've been here all night."

Releasing a huffing breath, Roth sat up. With his back against the heavy wooden headboard, he quirked an eyebrow at her.

"I know it's morning. If the sunshine trying to blind me through the sliver of an opening in the curtains wasn't a clue, the time on the clock did the job."

With an offended expression, he tugged at the sheet she gripped to her chest. Of course, she was no match for his strength, so the soft fabric gave way, revealing her bare breasts. In the full light of day, she was more self-conscious than when he'd undressed her the previous night.

"As for you still being here. In my bed. I'm also fully aware of that fact."

Leveling her with an expression she couldn't read beyond what she thought might be irritation, he continued with his assessment.

"The question is, why does it seem like it's suddenly a problem for you to be here with *me*?"

His query bounced inside Autumn's head along with what he didn't say. He'd asked her plainly last night what she wanted. She'd had no problems with any of it. Honestly, she wouldn't change a moment of it.

However, in the light of day, reality reared its head like a snake poking out from a burrow ready to strike. She'd spent the night with Roth. She hadn't called or messaged even one person to let them know about it. And while her sex life was none of their business, she was staying with her grandmother during her time back in Lone Star Ridge. Anyone with a Southern grandma knew, not only do you not come into her house at all times of the night, you most definitely do not spend the entire night out without giving her the courtesy of a phone call.

Her eyes had to be as round as saucers when she looked at Roth, because his expression shifted to one of concern. Whatever he'd been gearing up to say seemed to be pushed aside as he watched her face.

"Heeey..." His voice was noticeably softer as he pulled her to him, wrapping his arms around her. "What's going on, Sugar? You look like you've seen a ghost."

"I didn't tell anyone where I was going when we left the event last night."

Tucking her head beneath his chin, she curled into his body seeking warmth and protection.

"Okay..."

"Roth, I've been staying with Grandma Hattie since I've been home. Remember?"

Roth's entire body went rigid beneath her. Although both sets of his grandparents were no longer living, he'd been close to her grandparents and now her grandmother since her grandfather passed not long after his. Not calling her nearly ninety-year-old grandmother to let her know she was safe, was going to go over like a ton of bricks.

Two light taps to her hip preceded him nearly lifting her from the bed and hustling her into the bathroom.

"Come on, Sugar. We need to get you back to Miss Hattie's. It's still early. Maybe she's not up yet."

As unlikely as it was that her grandmother wasn't awake at six a.m. on a Sunday morning, Autumn clung to the sliver of hope Roth presented. Unlike when they'd shared a shower the previous evening, there were no slips of the hand or accidental bumps leading to intentional slips and bumps. Autumn almost felt like she'd joined the military with the efficiency Roth used to bathe first her then himself before hopping out of the shower to dry them both off.

While she was attempting to wrangle her hair into a semblance of something which didn't look like she'd been doing exactly what she'd been doing all night, Roth left the bathroom. He returned with her clothes and clutch purse. Reaching into the linen closet, he produced a toothbrush still in the packaging.

"Amelia is big on not running out of things." he explained as he opened it for her.

"I guess I owe her a thank you," Autumn murmured.

Accepting the offering, she made quick work of cleaning her teeth after slipping her dress on. While she brushed, Roth zipped the gown. The entire moment felt as if they were a real couple—one who had been together for so long they were comfortable in one another's space. When she was done, he folded her hand into his and they walked downstairs.

In the time it had taken her to fuss with her hair, brush her teeth and slip into her dress, he'd donned a plaid button down and tucked it into the waist band of jeans which fit him like sin. He also held his hat in one hand. When they reached the door, he helped her into her heels before shoving his feet into his boots.

The drive to her grandmother's house took less than twenty minutes since the Daley property bordered the Stephens' ranch on one side. Crossing the little stream separating their properties was quicker when traveling on horse or foot, but in a vehicle, they had to drive around.

Autumn tried not to fidget during the ride. It was possible she could have the answers to soothe her anxiety if she looked at her phone to check her messages. But, she didn't. She was putting off facing that particular reality as long as she could.

When Roth turned his truck onto the long driveway leading up to the house, Autumn suddenly realized how loud the vehicle was. It may as well have been an army tank rumbling up to the front door of her grandmother's home. Sighing, she just looked out the window. There was nothing that could be done about it now.

Once the behemoth rolled to a stop, Roth put it in park and cut the engine.

"What are you doing?" With one hand on the door, she raked her gaze over him.

"I'm gonna walk you to the door."

"You absolutely are not! It's bad enough that I've been out all night without a call. Having you walk me to the door will simply add fuel to the fire."

Although not the fire Autumn spoke of, the heat which blazed to life in Roth's eyes was just as hot.

"I'm not gonna just drop you off and drive away, Sugar."

Letting go of the door handle, Autumn wrapped imploring fingers around Roth's forearm.

"Please, Roth. Please. Just do this my way. Grandma Hattie might still be sleeping. If she is, I don't want to disturb her."

"How is me walking you to the front door gonna disturb her sleep? I'm big, but I ain't a clomping Clydesdale. I know how not to stomp around making a ruckus."

She was certain after his years as an Army Ranger he was very adept at moving silently. Still...she didn't want to risk it.

"Let's say you come to the door with me and we don't wake Grandma Hattie—she's already awake. Then what? Are you coming in for breakfast? Are you also going to tell her why you're bringing me to her doorstep early in the morning after I've been out all night?"

Autumn watched as Roth mentally cycled through her questions. Never once had she ever considered him to be anything but brave. This moment included. However, she didn't need him to be brave right now. She needed him to drive this monster away from her grandma's front porch and let her try to sneak in the back way with some dignity. After a stare down which seemed to last forever, Roth finally nodded.

"Fine. We'll do it your way." Piercing her with a stern expression, he wrapped his thick fingers around the back of her neck, pulling her closer. "This time. And this time only, Sugar."

Punctuating his promise wrapped in a warning with kiss, he reminded her of where he stood. While brief, his exploration of her mouth was thorough before he released her with a parting peck. Reaching over her, he pushed the door open and unbuckled her seat belt before settling back in his seat.

"Go on inside before I change my mind."

Slightly dazed, Autumn accepted the gift. Grabbing the side of the truck, she stepped down and began the trek around the side of the house to the entrance right off the kitchen. If she was lucky, she could make it up the back stairs and to her room without running into her grandmother. As she rounded the corner, she looked back to see Roth still sitting in the cab of the truck watching her. Giving him a smile and a wave, she kept moving before she got it into her head to run back to him and spend the day in his bed.

Autumn felt really good about her chances after she turned the knob on the back door and it opened without so much as a squeak. The thing usually creaked or moaned like it required constant oiling. The only way to keep the noise down was to move glacially slow when opening it. Closing the door behind her slowly, she tip-toed on bare feet, carrying her shoes in her hand. She had just stepped on the second stair when she learned luck was not on her side.

"Little girl, why are you trying to sneak into my house fo-day in the morning? And what is Rothschild Stephens doing parked in my front yard?"

Autumn's entire being deflated. Her shoulders dropped and her head hung low enough for her chin to graze her chest. Not only was she caught, Roth hadn't left. So, it was likely they'd both have to face the wrath of Grandma Hattie.

Chapter Nine

Roth watched Autumn walk around the corner of her grandparent's ranch house. Made on a similar style to the one he lived in, he was aware of the location of the door, which was hidden from view where he was parked. However, only the curtains on the windows prevented him from seeing inside. It didn't matter. He knew what was there.

He'd spent many days hanging out with Nick at Sunset ranch. Countless meals were had at the very table he'd bet money Miss Hattie was sitting at this very moment. His promise to Autumn was the only thing keeping his ass in the driver's seat of his truck. But he didn't like her going in there alone. Not even a little.

Had it not been for the call from Chuck, they'd likely still be wrapped around each other in his bed. For some reason, the foreman hadn't expected Roth to follow through with his commitment to take the weekend off. Likely because he hadn't in the past, and mostly because he'd still gone out to do some chores before he left them to get ready for the charity auction.

Honestly, if he hadn't awakened with Autumn wrapped

in his arms, he probably would've been out with the rest of the weekend crew checking on the cattle. Then, he would've seen for himself where Titan had damaged a section of the fence separating two pastures. It was likely due to a female in heat wandering too close to the barrier and the stud bull was trying to get to them.

Since he'd put the cattle on a specific rotation for calving, they kept Titan and the other stud bulls away from the females during certain seasons. Apparently, the cantankerous bull didn't appreciate the separation.

Roth was going to suggest moving the herd to another pasture, but Chuck was already on it. He'd sequestered Titan for the time being, so they could keep their schedule for rotating the cows without interference from him. That's what they get for letting him roam around the pasture so long in the first place. Since Chuck had the relocation under control, Roth told him to put Titan on the schedule. Maybe if the bull had some time with cows in need of servicing, he wouldn't try breaking through gates.

Roth couldn't blame the bull though. He felt a bit like bursting through a gate or two when Autumn walked away from him. It was almost like being with her had unleashed something he'd kept locked down inside himself. But maybe it was inevitable.

They'd actually never been alone the way they were the previous night. And he'd most definitely never had her soft curves pressed against him like they were when he carried her to his truck. The desires he'd suppressed following her *almost wedding* came back with a vengeance. The only person who could've stopped it was Autumn. When she encouraged him, she sealed her fate.

He'd considered himself too broken to be of good to anyone in a relationship. Although his time with Andy at Silver Creek had helped him heal tremendously, Roth hadn't wanted to saddle anyone with his issues. The trauma from the mission, which prompted his early retirement, reared its head randomly.

The last thing he wanted was to burden another person with his unexplainable mood swings—he didn't want to even think about the nightmares. But when he did, he recalled how peacefully he slept with her in his arms. For the first time in forever, he slept more than four hours straight and didn't wake up drenched in sweat.

Movement near the curtains drew Roth's gaze, and he knew there was no way he was leaving Sunset Ranch without going inside. He'd told his Sugar they'd do it her way, but it looked like things had been taken out of both their hands. Plucking his keys from the cup holder in the center console, he considered grabbing his hat off the dashboard before deciding against it.

Stepping out of the truck, he didn't bother to lock up when he closed the door behind him. There was no one out this way to break into a vehicle. Everyone knew everyone. So, it was a non-issue.

Roth's stride was sure as he walked the same path Autumn had taken, stopping in front of the side door. Delivering two firm taps to the wooden frame instead of the glass pane, he waited for a response. It was a short wait. Less than a minute later, he was peering into her face. Her sullen expression was reminiscent of a scolded teenager instead the woman who'd boldly kissed him not twenty-four hours ago.

"Don't just stand there at the door looking at each other. Come on in here, Rothschild."

Mouthing, *I'm sorry*, Autumn stepped back to allow him inside. Sliding his arm around her waist, he dropped a quick kiss on her forehead.

"Don't worry about it, Sugar. I'll be fine."

His words were for her ears only, but it was clear Miss

Hattie heard them when he entered, closing the door behind him.

"Miss Hattie." He greeted her with a head tilt. His fingers reflexively reached for the brim of the hat he'd left in the truck.

"Mhm." Was her short response given through lightly pursed lips.

The aroma of fresh coffee, biscuits and bacon permeated the spacious kitchen. It was more than obvious Autumn's grandmother had been awake, and busy, for quite some time.

"You two go wash up. Breakfast is ready."

Having spent more than half of his life following the instruction of the Daley matriarch, Roth offered no objection as he followed Autumn to the powder room located in the hallway just off the kitchen. The second they were out of Miss Hattie's direct line of sight, he tugged Autumn closer to him.

"Are you okay, Sugar? You look a tad like a whipped dog."

"Gee, thanks."

"Come on, Sugar. Don't be like that. You know what I mean."

Turning on the water, Roth tried to buy them a little time. Rotating her toward him with his hands on her shoulders, he searched her face.

"Talk to me."

With a shrug, she attempted to avoid his stare. "I'm fine. She hasn't said anything I didn't expect." Finally, she looked directly into his eyes. "Why didn't you leave? I thought we agreed?"

"I agreed not to come in with you, not to immediately drive away. But that option was taken off the table when I saw your grandma through the window. There was no way I was going home to let you face her alone."

"I'm fine, Roth. You don't have to be a white knight riding to my rescue."

"Well, that's good. Because if I was a knight, I'd definitely wear black—or Army green."

Her push against his shoulder was halfhearted, but his lips tipped up with the corresponding curve of hers.

"I can't with you."

"Sure you can, Sugar. Now, wash your hands before Miss Hattie comes looking for us. We'll talk more later."

While Roth only partially believed her when she said she was fine, he knew they didn't have an indefinite amount of time before her grandmother had something to say about how long it was taking them to perform the quick task of washing their hands.

When they returned to the kitchen the formerly empty farmhouse style table was now laden with more food than the three of them could possibly eat. Even with Roth's hefty appetite, there was bound to be leftovers.

"Thank you, Child."

Miss Hattie's murmur of thanks when he helped her with her chair was his first indicator that maybe things wouldn't go as poorly as Autumn thought. She'd shifted from using his full name to the shortened version only she and a select few others were allowed to use.

"You're welcome."

Autumn's hand on the back of her own chair drew a grunt of disapproval from Roth.

"Don't."

A line appeared between her eyebrows, but she took her hand off the chair. Ignoring her disgruntled stare, Roth rounded the table, tugged the chair out and looked at her expectantly. With a little sniff, she accepted his assistance. Once she was seated, he bent low to whisper in her ear.

"You know better than to pull out your own chair in the presence of a man, Sugar."

She didn't respond. But, he didn't expect it. A thought

briefly floated across his mind, wondering what kind of men she'd dealt with in Nevada where she'd suddenly forgotten what it was like to have someone take care of her. Even if it wasn't him, he knew her brother, father and cousins had all been taught the same. Roth had witnessed it.

Following the blessing of the food, they ate quietly for a few moments. Roth was contemplating another biscuit, this time slathered with fresh apple butter instead of jam, when Miss Hattie broke the silence.

"You two are grown and can do what you want, but you need to know if you were planning to keep this thing between you a secret, that chicken has flown the coop."

Roth was grateful he didn't have anything in his mouth when she spoke, but Autumn wasn't so lucky. The orange juice she just sipped was only prevented from splattering onto her plate by the hand she clamped over her mouth. Hastily grabbing a napkin, she dabbed at the wetness on her face before cleaning her fingers.

"Grandma!"

"What? You act like I said something scandalous." Miss Hattie sat back in her chair, gently patting her lips with a napkin. "I'm simply warning you. It's like I told you before Child came in here, what you do as a grown woman isn't my business. But, you're staying in my house. So, I expect the courtesy of a phone call when you don't come home. That way I won't wait up for you or picture you lying in a ditch somewhere."

Autumn's shoulders slumped. Roth knew the not-so-gentle reminder of their failure to let her grandmother know she was safe and was sleeping elsewhere for the night had hit home. He was sideswiped by it himself. It never occurred to him to ask where she was expected to be before he kept her at his place all night.

"I'm sorry, Grandma."

"Don't be sorry. Do better." Flicking her napkin to open it back up, she placed it in her lap once more. "Now, how are you planning to handle your parents and your brother?"

Roth glimpsed Autumn giving her own napkin hell, twisting it in her lap. Placing one hand over both of hers, he squeezed her fingers.

"Grandma, it's like you said. We're grown. I don't see where what happens between us needs to be discussed with Mama, Daddy, or Nick."

"Bless your heart..."

In his periphery, Roth saw the older woman shake her head. He was staring at Autumn in disbelief. While he didn't think it would be a pleasant conversation between him and Nick, he did feel a discussion was due. Because, he'd be damned if he hid, and he sure as hell wasn't going to stop now that he'd tasted her sweetness. Not gonna happen.

"What?" Autumn looked between the two of them wearing an expression which let him know she fully believed what she'd said.

"Baby girl... Number one, no matter how grown you are, being as Child and Nick have been friends since before they started smelling themselves, y'all are gonna have to tell him something. Now, your mama probably has her fingers and toes crossed hoping she gets to plan a wedding. As for your daddy..."

She stopped and leveled a serious look toward Roth. "He's gonna wanna have a talk with Child about his intentions—especially considering he just spent a hundred thousand dollars for a date with you."

Shit. So much had happened since he'd made that bid at the charity auction, Roth didn't even think about it. He completely ignored Miss Hattie's remark about a wedding when she mentioned the money for the date.

"Grandma, I understand what you're saying, but why do I have to think about any of that right now?"

"Because, Tum-tum. When you didn't show up by midnight, I called your phone. When I didn't get an answer, I called Travis and Carla, since you left here with them. I was giving them hell about not telling me you were staying the night at their house when they told me you'd left early with Child."

As if their life had suddenly turned into one of the television dramas his mother was crazy about, the distinct sound of a vehicle approaching drew their attention to the now open curtains. Before anyone stepped out of the champagne-colored sport utility vehicle, Roth already knew who it was. Also, the amount of food Miss Hattie cooked now made sense.

Chapter Ten

Autumn followed Roth's gaze to the window and her stomach dropped to her feet. This couldn't possibly be happening. It was bad enough she was caught trying to slip into the house like a child who missed curfew. Now, her parents and her brother were about to see her still wearing the dress she had on last night. It wouldn't take skilled calculations to determine why she wasn't at least in her pajamas, if not something appropriate for church.

The comfort she'd drawn from Roth's warm hand covering hers began to evaporate. Hearing Grandma Hattie say she'd called around when Autumn didn't come home, simultaneously filled her with guilt and dread. She hadn't fully wrapped her own mind around what the night she'd spent with Roth meant. And now, she'd be forced to confront it in front of her very invasive family.

Considering everything she was going through at work, which had driven her into taking a sabbatical in the first place, the last thing she expected when she returned home was additional drama. The little appetite she had vanished, as she waited for the rest of her family to enter the kitchen. Instead of using the side entrance as she and Roth had done, they went to the front door.

Family rarely, if ever, knocked. So, footfalls were the warning signal before Nick appeared framed in the doorway. If Autumn was wondering what he thought, the scowl he directed toward Roth gave her all the answers she needed. Releasing the napkin she'd been twisting into a knot, she flipped her fingers, tangling them with Roth's in her lap. The reassuring squeeze from his strong hand offered her some comfort.

"Good morning, Mother Daley!"

Autumn's mother practically floated into the room, brushing Nick aside. Stopping next to her mother-in-law, she leaned in placing a kiss on the older woman's upturned cheek.

"Autumn. Roth. Good morning to you both as well."

Autumn wasn't sure how to process the saccharine sweet smile on her mother's face. But she wasn't given time to wonder as her mother flitted across the kitchen toward the powder room.

"Y'all started breakfast without us. Let me go wash up, and I'll join you."

Autumn noted that her brother didn't step farther inside until her dad stopped next to him and tapped his shoulder. He stopped to give his mother a kiss, just as his wife had done, before following the same path. When Autumn's mother returned, Roth stood to help her with her chair while Nick remained hovering by the doorway—just staring.

"Nicholas Joseph Daley, I suggest you go wash up and come sit instead of standing in my kitchen like you don't have manners."

With their grandma pulling out his full name, Nick finally moved more than a step into the room. His stoic demeanor did nothing to make Autumn feel better about the pending conversation which was bound to occur once her parents were back. Nick used the kitchen sink to wash his hands instead of following their parents. By the time he was done, they were rounding the corner.

The seconds ticked by turning into minutes as her father dished food onto a plate for her mother before serving himself. Although Nick had an empty plate in front of him, he didn't bother to put food on it. He also declined the coffee their mother offered him when she poured her own. When her parents said nothing, Autumn wasn't certain what was happening. After they commenced eating their breakfast, as if this were any other Sunday morning, she was thoroughly confused.

She was considering excusing herself to at least go change clothes when her mother broke the silence. Once she opened her mouth, Autumn would wish a thousand-fold she'd remained quiet.

"So, where are you two thinking of going on your date?"

"You mean Roth didn't get his money's worth last night?"

Her brother's words had barely pierced the air before Roth shot to his feet. Nick popped up from his seat as well, the swift movement nearly toppling his chair over.

"Nicholas Daley!" Their mother's horrified screech mingled with their father's thundering admonishment.

Tears sprang to Autumn's eyes. So shocked by Nick's callous words, she was surprised she had the presence of mind to grab onto Roth's arm. Beneath her fingers, his tightly coiled muscles felt like granite.

"You wanna be mad? Be mad. But don't you dare speak about your sister that way."

The deadly calm of Roth's voice belied the tension in his stance and the fire in his gaze as he stared at Nick.

"Oh. So, now you remember that she's my sister?"

"What's that supposed to mean?"

Roth's body tilted forward with his question, prompting Autumn to jump to her feet, maintaining her hold on his arm.

"What do you think it means? You two snuck away last night. She still has on the same dress. And, from what Grandma Hattie says, she didn't come home."

"Don't go throwing my name around like I'm going to stand behind you showing your ass, Nicholas."

Their grandmother's remark was quickly followed by their father intervening.

"Son, that's enough. Sit down."

For a moment Autumn thought Nick wouldn't obey their dad's instruction. Her brother continued to glare at Roth, who returned the expression with equal heat.

"I said, sit your ass down. Both of you."

The steel in their father's voice finally seemed to break the standoff. Nick straightened his chair before sitting. Roth didn't sit until he'd helped Autumn return to her seat.

"Sorry for cussing, Mama." Her father's voice was gruff, but contrite when he apologized to his mother.

Grandma Hattie waved a dismissive hand before giving Nick her full attention.

"I agree with Child. You can be mad all you want, but I better not ever hear you disrespecting your sister like that again. Not to mention the rest of us."

"Nana—"

"Don't Nana me. You were wrong, and you know it. I've already said my piece to Autumn and whatever your parents have to say, I'm sure they will. But, what isn't going to happen is you implying that your sister sold herself, and your *friend* of almost thirty years paid for the privilege of being with her. It's not who we are, and I won't stand for it. Do you understand me?"

Although it was easy to detect Nick fuming beneath the surface, Autumn noted he reined himself in. Dipping his head in acknowledgement wasn't enough for their grandmother.

"You were man enough to be insulting aloud. Let everything else be just as loud."

Clearing his throat, with obvious difficulty, Nick responded. "Yes, ma'am. I understand."

With a stiff nod, Grandma Hattie picked up her fork and stabbed the homestyle potatoes on her plate. Her return to eating meant the discussion was closed. She wouldn't make him apologize. Their family didn't believe in apologies unless you meant it. So, Nick would have to come to it in his own time.

Autumn still had no interest in food, but she didn't move from the table. With one hand clasped around hers, Roth picked up his fork and finished off the last of what was on his plate.

From the way he forked it into his mouth, it appeared he did it out of obligation, not actual enjoyment. Stealing a glance at her mother, Autumn encountered her stare. Her soft expression eased a portion of Autumn's anxiety. She was thankful the expected interrogation didn't occur, because she had no set answers. No discussion surrounding a future, be it near or far, had been held.

While she was hopeful what occurred between her and Roth would extend beyond one night or a limited time, there were a lot of moving pieces. The major one, beyond the dust up with Nick, was they resided in two separate states with more than a thousand miles between them.

Autumn doubted very seriously he had any interest in giving up his ranch to relocate to the Las Vegas area. And, despite her current situation with her job, she wasn't certain if she was ready to say that phase of her life was over. She needed time to figure it out.

The only conversation at the table was between her mother and grandmother. Autumn's mama was filling Grandma Hattie in on what she missed by not attending the charity auction. Thankfully, she didn't dwell on Roth's show-stopping gesture when he bid on a date with Autumn. Although, she couldn't seem to stop herself from mentioning it was the largest donation of the night.

"That was very generous of you, Child."

Roth only nodded in acknowledgement of her grandma's praise. When he abruptly released her hand, Autumn was startled by how bereft she felt as a result of his warm fingers no longer being wrapped around hers. The reason for the release was quickly evident when he gathered the remainder of her untouched food, stacking her plate on top of his before rising with both in his hands.

"You don't have to do that, Roth." Autumn moved to take the dishes from him.

"Don't worry about it, Sugar. I've got it."

Nick's audible huff following the endearment earned him a glare from more than just Autumn. The flutter in her stomach wasn't the same as the one she experienced when he first made the shift to calling her *Sugar*. This was more anxious, because his use of it in front of her family spoke volumes. In all the years they'd known one another, the only nickname he'd ever used for her was Tummy. Him dropping the use of her family nickname in front of them... It made her realize their conversation needed to happen sooner rather than later.

However, her plans were waylaid when her father stood from the table performing tasks similar to what Roth had done for Autumn. Tilting his head toward Nick, he motioned for her brother to take their grandmother's plate as the men cleared the table.

"Why don't you ladies go on into the living room? We've got this covered."

Her dad's suggestion wasn't actually a suggestion. Autumn's nervous glance toward Roth was met with a resolute expression and a similar head tilt. His eyes projected exactly what he expected from her. So, she reluctantly followed her mother and grandma from the kitchen.

Part of her wanted to hang back to hear the conversation between the men. Autumn wasn't under the illusion her dad sending them from the room wasn't a cover for him wanting to speak to Roth without them around.

The moment they stepped into the hallway, she quickly excused herself, bolting up the stairs. She didn't pause to consider the oddity of neither woman objecting. Since she'd showered at Roth's place, her wardrobe change was quick. When she came back down the stairs, she paused at the bottom, after hearing the low rumble of male voices.

It was quite likely she would've stayed there trying to eavesdrop if her mama hadn't poked her head out of the living room, giving Autumn a pointed look. Not nearly as embarrassed as she should've been at being discovered, she left the stairs to join the other women.

Entering the space, she was struck by how silent they were. Her steps slowed as her gaze pinged between them. Her mother was seated on the sofa next to her grandma, but neither was speaking. *What in the world was going on? Was this when they interrogated her? While her dad and Nick had Roth isolated in the kitchen?*

Before she could form the right questions to get ahead of what she thought was coming, her mother waved her over with one hand while she pressed the finger of the other to her lips. It didn't take long for Autumn to realize why her mama wanted her to stay quiet.

The voices, which were a low rumble when she was on the stairs, were much clearer. Autumn's eyes widened as understanding dawned on her. This was why they hadn't complained when her dad sent them to the other room. And, why they didn't say a word about her sprinting away to change clothes. They'd been eavesdropping this entire time.

Chapter Eleven

Only his respect for Miss Hattie and Autumn's parents kept Roth from doing more than glaring at his life-long friend. He hadn't expected Nick to want to throw a party when he figured out Roth and Autumn had spent the night together. Nick was smart, so he quickly connected the dots. But he apparently hated the picture they formed.

Tough shit. Roth wouldn't cheapen what happened between him and Autumn. He also had every intention of doing it again. Regularly. If she'd have him. Considering her response to him, it was unlikely she'd turn him away.

Going about the task of dumping Autumn's uneaten breakfast into the trash, Roth waited for what he knew was coming. Travis Daley wasn't a man who wasted words. So, Roth knew he'd say what he wanted to say when he was ready —not a moment sooner.

It wasn't necessary to look at Nick, Roth felt his friend's stare boring into his back as he moved around the kitchen. He was thankful for the spaciousness of the area. It meant they didn't have to get close to one another. Roth was still fuming over the things Nick said. If he got too close, he couldn't promise they wouldn't *accidentally* bump into each other.

After a few minutes, Mr. Daley stopped moving around. Standing in front of the island containing a butcher block countertop, he folded his arms across his chest. Roth flicked the handle on the faucet to stop the flow of water into the sink. Miss Hattie had a dishwasher, but he knew she didn't like it. So, it didn't occur to him to do anything other than prepare to hand wash the plates and cutlery.

"How long has this thing been going on between you and Autumn?"

Mr. Daley's voice was calm and the question was delivered without the edge of harshness. However, it didn't sound any less accusatory.

"Respectfully, sir. It sounds as if you think Autumn and I have been secretly seeing each other behind your back."

"Have you?" Nick spit out the question before his father could respond to Roth's statement.

Cutting a glare at Nick, Roth worked to keep his temper in check. Flying off the handle wouldn't help the situation. If he hadn't been reared to be respectful of his elders, and didn't have such a close relationship with the Daley family, this entire conversation wouldn't even be a consideration. However, this was his life and current condition.

Ignoring Nick's question, Roth returned his stare to Mr. Daley. He'd deal with his friend later. With a shrug, the older man slightly tilted his head toward Nick.

"My son has a valid question, and you still haven't answered mine."

Folding his own arms, Roth leaned against the counter with the sink behind him.

"Last night was the first time I've seen Autumn for more than an hour in years. Not since she moved to Nevada. So, no. We haven't been sneaking around behind anyone's back."

Nick grunted as if he didn't believe Roth. It was on the tip of Roth's tongue to remind them both that he and Autumn were consenting adults. There was no need for sneaking and secrecy. And, despite their close family ties, they weren't related. So, no kissing or any other kind of cousins was in play.

Roth couldn't say it didn't sting just a bit for his life-long friend to suddenly treat him as if he was a fuck boy preying on Autumn's innocence. While it wasn't their business to know, as special as the previous night was, he wasn't her first. And she wasn't his. He also wouldn't tell them it was Autumn kissing him that started the ball rolling. Again. That wasn't their business to know and he wouldn't be the one to tell them.

Unlike Nick, Mr. Daley's face was unreadable as he stared at Roth. Finally, he asked the question Roth anticipated the moment he saw them through the window.

"Rothschild, you and Nick have been friends for so long, I've grown to see you as another son. But, Autumn is my only daughter, and I won't have her toyed with. She's had enough of that to last a lifetime. So, what are your intentions?"

"Sir, I'd *never* toy with Autumn." Dropping his arms, Roth rested the heel of his palms against the edge of the sink behind him. "So, my intentions are honorable. But I won't say anything more than that until she and I have a chance to talk about it."

Nick's scoff quickly followed Roth's statement. "You won't say more, but you'll all but say y'all spent the night doing everything but talking. Like that's some shit we needed to know."

The heat of anger licked up Roth's neck, causing his composure to slip.

"What the fuck is your problem, man? You're talking about *your sister.*"

Roth heard the growling note in his own voice. He hadn't

even realized he moved until Mr. Daley's hand landed in the center of his chest to keep him from stepping completely into Nick's space. Glaring at his so-called friend, Roth searched his face.

"You're acting like you haven't known me for most of my life. Like we haven't fought shoulder to shoulder and watched each other's backs for years. Is the thought of me having more than a passing interest in Autumn such a terrible thing?"

Regardless of what Nick said, Roth knew he couldn't walk away from Autumn. Not even to save his friendship.

"That *is* my problem man. *I know* you. I know things about you Autumn probably never will. You actually expect me to be okay with you being with my sister? My *sister*? I'm not."

Spinning on his heel as if he'd been commanded during drills, Nick showed Roth his back as he exited the kitchen. A few seconds later, the sound of the front door opening and closing reverberated through the house.

If Nick had punched Roth in the face, it couldn't have had more of an impact. He wasn't completely wrong. They'd grown up together. Nick knew things about Roth even his family didn't know. It was due partially to their friendship and their time serving together as Rangers.

While Roth knew he'd had a stretch of time where he was really fucked up. And honestly, he was still dealing with some of those things. Having his friend insinuate the stuff he'd done in the military and his struggles after giving up his commission made him unsuitable for Autumn stung. More than a little.

For Roth, those could be the only references for Nick to point to. He'd had a few relationships, but they hadn't ended because he treated the woman poorly. Usually, it was due to him being exactly who he told them he was, a career military man who wasn't in the market for a wife. Someone always thought they'd be the one to change his mind.

He'd transitioned to mutually beneficial arrangements long before he ever left the service. It was much easier for all involved. Until he'd seen Autumn again, and actually touched her, Roth hadn't considered a future. With her or anyone else. But, he'd known the moment he let things get past kissing, there was no stopping this train.

Mr. Daley pulled Roth from his thoughts when he dropped his hand and retook his position in front of the island. To his credit, he didn't make excuses for Nick or try to convince Roth that Nick hadn't meant what he said.

"Son, I can respect your position. But you need to appreciate mine. Like I said, Autumn is my only daughter. And you were there for the mess with that piece of shit on her wedding day. So, you know she's already been through a rough time. Even with her leaving the state, it took her a while to get over it."

Nodding, Roth returned to his spot in front of the sink and matched the older man's pose when he leaned against the edge.

"This thing with you has the potential to hurt her far worse than Russell ever could. Because as much as she thought she loved him, she didn't know him the way she knows you. Did either of you consider how much our families are intertwined?

My wife and your mother are friends. They socialize in the same circles. Hell, your father and I play golf together twice a month. What happens when whatever this is you two are doing goes sideways?"

While Mr. Daley didn't say it, to Roth, his words didn't only imply the imminent demise of his budding relationship with Autumn, but that he would be the reason for it. It's quite possible he was overly sensitive to being blamed because of Nick's outburst. However, Roth couldn't stop himself from drawing that conclusion.

Somehow, he managed to keep his voice level when he responded. "Like I said, sir. Before I speak on it with anyone else, Autumn and I need to talk. But you should know, I'd never do anything to hurt her. And I'm not planning for there to be a mess for anyone to clean up."

Mr. Daley stared at him silently for another few moments before nodding. Understanding the discussion was over, at least temporarily, Roth turned toward the sink, turning on the hot water to resume his task. He'd just placed the first clean plate onto the drying rack when Mr. Daley spoke again.

"I know you believe yourself to be a man of honor, and you've never shown me any different. That being said, I will always choose my child's well-being over anyone else's. You keep that in mind."

Roth didn't look up or pause in his movements. A second later, he noted Autumn's father had left the room from the sound of his retreating footsteps. A few moments after that, softer footfalls reached his ears. He felt Autumn's presence before he saw her in his periphery.

"Hey, Sugar. How are you feeling?"

Her soft fingers curled against his forearm and he stopped moving to fully look at her. Her dark brown eyes appeared bottomless as she stared up at him.

"I'm fine." She applied pressure on his arm until he stopped moving. Her bottom lip disappeared between her teeth briefly, then she released it. "I'm sorry. About this morning. About Nick. All of it."

Her voice was barely above a whisper, so he had to lean in to hear her. Roth immediately shook his head. Grabbing a towel, he dried his hands, pulling her into a hug.

"Sugar, you don't have to apologize. You didn't do anything wrong. There's no way you could've known any of this would happen."

Nuzzling her hair, he kissed her forehead when he tilted

her face up toward his. Deciding not to push the envelope, he avoided her deliciously pouty lips. Her amazing curves were a test of his will pressed against him, but he managed to keep things PG.

"Don't worry about Nick. We'll work it out. There's nothing for you to do there."

The cloud of concern in her dark eyes made him squeeze her closer.

"I'm serious, Sugar. I'll handle it."

Roth wasn't sure how he'd deliver on his promise, but he knew he'd get it done. Having tension with his best friend because he'd yielded to his own desires wasn't something he relished. He didn't delve into the reality of what he felt for Autumn being beyond simple desire.

One bite at a time. It was the only way to eat a two-thousand-pound bull. One bite at a time.

Chapter Twelve

Autumn rubbed her eyes in an attempt to wipe away the weariness. She'd been staring at her computer screen for hours, researching case law and comparing them to the notes she'd taken. Sunset was no longer a large-scale ranch as it had been in the past, but there were still ranch hands taking care of the livestock and the land which hadn't been leased out to ranchers boarding the property.

The business was folded under the umbrella of her father's company, and Autumn happened to be visiting the offices when she sat in on a meeting where the smaller holdings were being discussed. Technically, the company was hers and Nick's but she'd been reluctant to move back home, and her brother enjoyed military life too much to give it up for the corporate world.

With her shares, she didn't actually need her job with Fortune Innovations in Las Vegas. If she even mentioned issues in the workplace, her father was quick to remind her there would always be a position for her with the Daley Group. But, Autumn wanted to make her own way. And she had. Which is why when the division head mentioned an issue regarding the foreman and problems with their insurance provider honoring the policy terms, her ears perked up.

She didn't specialize in medical or insurance issues, but she'd felt compelled to look into it. The legal department wasn't likely to take up the case due to their current load, and the employee couldn't afford the fees for an attorney skilled enough to make the insurance company rethink their position.

Low level vibrations on the desk, where her elbows rested, drew Autumn's attention to her cellphone. It was face down on the surface, so she had to flip it over to see the message from Roth.

Dinner at 6 p.m.

The smile that took over her face lifted her cheeks so high they nearly closed her eyes. She quickly tapped out a response.

Is that a request or a demand?

Propping her chin on her hand, she watched the screen, waiting for his reply. She enjoyed pushing his buttons. The payoff never failed to bring pleasure. Without conscious thought, she wiggled her bottom in the executive chair of her borrowed office.

The wi-fi at her grandma's house needed an upgrade in the worst way. Autumn had arranged for it. But for some reason, it was taking them forever to get out there. In the interim, she was using an unoccupied office at the Daley Group headquarters.

Roth had offered his place, but with the way they couldn't keep their hands off each other, that option was a non-starter. Her parent's house was out of the question, because then she'd have to field questions from her mama about her budding relationship with Roth.

Her phone vibrated again with a new message.

> Sugar, if you want a spanking, just say that. Have your sweet ass where I can see it no later than 5:55 p.m.

Autumn giggled around the hand she placed over her mouth as the next message came in.

> And you can take that whatever way results in you being where you're supposed to be when you're supposed to be there.

> So bossy. Does this count as our charity date? I thought you were supposed to take me somewhere nice.

> Sugar...

Autumn considered keeping things going, but she decided against it. She'd done enough to ensure she received proper...punishment for her behavior.

> 6:02. Got it.

> Gonna spank that ass, Sugar. Now go back to saving the day.

Autumn wiggled again at the warmth flooding her center from Roth's promise. She'd honestly never thought she was the kind of woman who enjoyed a well-executed spanking. But, where Roth was concerned, she'd learned there were very few limits on what she wouldn't try at least once.

She'd feel some type of way about it, however the same seemed to be true for him. As rough and gruff as he appeared on the exterior and in his speech, he'd been more than willing to explore with her in and out of the bedroom.

Also, she was now able to tease him about the charity date without thinking of the nasty way Nick made it sound. Fortunately, for her relationship with her brother, Nick had reached out to her to apologize for the things he'd said that morning over breakfast. He and Roth had come a long way since that morning. Neither of them would tell her what was said, but they had at least reached an impasse. Her brother returned to his base a few days later. But not before making a trip to the Lazy Creek.

Following his visit, Autumn wasn't subtle when she checked Roth over for even a hint of bruising. Her inspection was derailed due to an uncooperative subject, who turned things around on her until she was screaming herself hoarse from the explosive orgasms he delivered. Following that day, they never discussed Nick's visit again.

It was a struggle to refocus on wading through legalese after having her libido awakened by Roth's message, but Autumn managed. When her watch eventually buzzed, letting her know it was time to call it a day, she was more than ready.

Although she was a couple of hours early, she opted to drive to Roth's place instead of Grandma Hattie's. Having learned her lesson the first night they spent together, she called her grandmother from the car as she drove out to the Lazy Creek. The call connected after only a few rings.

"Hello?" Her grandma's questioning hello sounded far away from the phone causing Autumn to frown.

"Granny? You sound like you're across the room from the phone. What's going on?"

"That's because I am across the room. I have bread dough on my hands. I was gonna clean them off, then I remembered you told me I could just tell Sara to answer the phone, and I wouldn't have to touch it."

Autumn squelched the giggle that rose within her at her

grandmother's reference to the built-in electronic assistant as Sara. She refused to call it anything else. It was a wonder the thing actually responded to any requests. But it did.

"Oh. Okay. Well, I was calling to check on you and let you know not to wait up for me tonight."

"You and that boy might as well move in together. You haven't spent more than two or three nights here ever since the morning he parked his truck in my yard. The only time you show up here is to get more clothes."

"Granny! I don't think that's true."

It was totally true, but Autumn couldn't believe her grandma called her out so blatantly.

"Listen, little girl. You can lie to yourself as much as you want, but don't bring it to me. I didn't get this old and learn nothing along the way."

Knowing there was no way she would win this round with Hattie Daley, Autumn simply changed the subject.

"Do you need anything? I can stop by the store or whatever."

Despite not laying her head at her Grandma Hattie's each night, Autumn did check on her every day and run errands for her. It was the least she could do while she was in Lone Star. It took some of the load off her parents since her grandmother refused to have anyone underfoot—which was how she felt about the companion they attempted to hire when she declined their invitation to move in with them a few years ago.

"No, baby. I'm okay. I'm just gonna make my bread, then have my dinner. I'll probably sit on the porch for a little while before I go on to bed."

"Okay. If you're sure." Autumn merged into the lane to take the highway as she prepared to end the call.

"Oh! I almost forgot."

"You almost forgot what, Granny?"

"You got a package today. I left it on the table in the hallway."

Autumn sat up straighter in the seat. "A package? From who?"

"Hmm... I don't recall the name, but it had a Las Vegas address on it. It was one of those big envelopes."

"Oh. Okay. Thanks. I'll get it in the morning. It's probably from Fortune."

"Are you sure? I can have one of the boys bring it over to you. You know at least two or three of them will come around as soon as they smell dinner."

"I'm sure. Whatever they want can wait. I'm not on their time right now."

Autumn was curious as to what the company would've deemed worthy to send a package, but she wouldn't alter her plans or potentially sour her day by opening anything from Fortune Innovations. At least not until tomorrow.

"If you say so."

"I do."

They chatted for a few more minutes before her grandma ended the call. She didn't give a reason, but she didn't really have to. Autumn had accomplished her goal. Also, with her grandma mentioning having one of the hands bring over the package, Autumn was now comforted in knowing someone was going to stop by and keep her grandma company. At least for as long as it took them to wolf down a meal.

As the turn off for the Lazy Creek came into view, her thoughts shifted to the man who'd occupied most of her time for the past few weeks. She allowed herself a moment to daydream about what it could be like if she decided not to return to Nevada. In a roundabout way, she'd discussed it with her closest friend, Kiara, when they'd last spoken.

Since she'd been back home and they couldn't see one another regularly, they exchanged text messages most days and an actual phone call once a week. Her bestie had been far from surprised Autumn and Roth finally hooked up, citing the fact that she had been drooling over him for years.

While they'd talked, Autumn hadn't brought it up to Roth. What they had was new. Tenuous. She didn't want to stress it with future talk when she was still uncertain of which direction she wanted to take her career.

Slowing the vehicle, she carefully navigated off the highway onto the road to the Lazy Creek, passing through the gates while looking at the livestock grazing in the field. Just as she was about to give the private road her full attention, she caught a glimpse of a figure in the distance.

Even from more than two hundred yards away, she recognized Roth sitting astride his favorite mount, Big Tex. The Shire horse was one of the few breeds able to handle the weight of a man as large as Roth. He and his brothers all had Draft Breed horses because of their size—the horses and the men.

Seeing him astride the big beast stirred something inside her beyond the usual lust. Being honest, it didn't take much for her to mount his big body and practice her equestrian skills. But seeing him in his element, moving through the cows at a light trot, it struck a different chord inside her.

Unwillingly, her thoughts went back to the package delivered to her grandmother's house. She was positive it was the work she'd taken her sabbatical to remove herself from. Autumn also had no doubt as to who would be bold enough to ignore the terms of her leave of absence to send it to her. Flint Childers. One of the senior staff attorneys at Fortune and a big part of the reason Autumn was considering leaving the company.

The man was the epitome of the phrase, it's not what you know, but who you know. As long as they'd been in separate legal divisions, Autumn had done well. Her reputation was stellar. Suddenly, when he transferred to Corporate Governance, everything she said had to be backed up with more case law, requiring additional paralegals assigned to research.

It was bullshit. But Flint wasn't the only catalyst for her sabbatical. She'd already been on the path to discontent at Fortune. Having Flint in her division was simply another hole poked in the boat already filling with water.

Chapter Thirteen

Lifting his hat, Roth swiped at the perspiration on his brow. The cloth he used barely made a difference with the way sweat was pouring off him. It was hot as hell under the bright Texas sun. With the high humidity and the sun scorching from above, they were trying to rotate the herds closer to the creek. Those in the northern pasture had already been watered. He was helping the hands with the stragglers in the southern pasture.

Some ranch owners weren't as hands on as he was, when the ranch was as large as the Lazy Creek. But, Roth enjoyed being involved in more than determining where to plant the best grazing grass and breeding cycles. More than he enjoyed it, he needed it. Some days, physically exhausting himself was the way he was reminded that he was still alive. That he'd survived and drew breath.

The only other thing which brought him the same measure of peace was the time he spent with Autumn. Since their first night together, they'd slept in the same bed more often than not. And, he actually *slept* with her. More soundly than he had in years. The nightmares, which used to wake him at least once a week, were mysteriously absent when she curved her body into his each night.

Over the low, intermittent vocalizations from the cattle, he couldn't hear much. Yet, he noticed the moment Autumn turned the silver SUV onto Lazy Creek Road. Dust kicked up from the gravel despite her driving slowly and carefully. Like him, she'd been taught not to speed down the road nearest grazing pastures. It wasn't uncommon for one of the cows to get through the fence and end up standing in the middle of the road.

Seeing her driving toward the main house took his thoughts toward the future and the past simultaneously. He knew what he wanted. Having his Sugar with him in Lone Star Ridge on a permanent basis. Roth wanted her to not simply extend her sabbatical, but turn in her notice, leaving Las Vegas behind. However, he hadn't asked her to do any of that. Mainly because he knew it was fast as hell for him to ask for such a commitment, but partially because of the quasi-promise he'd made to Nick. They'd finally talked before Nick returned to his post.

One Month Ago

Roth sat in the rocker on the front porch watching as the pickup truck in the distance drew closer to the house. He recognized the chrome on black Dually. When the vehicle was closer, his view of the person in the driver's seat confirmed it. It was Nick. The only time the truck moved farther than a few feet at a time was when he was in town.

Thankful that Autumn was busy with her mother, he planted both feet firmly on the wooden surface and waited. In a few minutes, Nick drove to a stop in front of the attached garage and cut the engine. The two stared at one another through the glass of the windshield but neither moved for an unmeasured amount of time.

Roth refused to be the one to make the first move and he was certain Nick probably felt the same. While in one aspect, he could see Nick's perspective. Autumn was his younger and only sister. He saw it as his duty to protect her. On the other, Roth was still pissed at Nick for the way he spoke about her and to her that morning.

It was something he'd never thought his friend would do. Although Roth had never mentioned to Nick anything regarding his interest in Autumn, he couldn't have predicted Nick's response, that he would say such mean-spirited things. Especially inferring that Roth was treating Autumn like a prostitute.

So, recalling how hurt Autumn was and had been following the incident, Roth didn't move a muscle. Instead, he held Nick's gaze until the other man looked away and climbed out of the cab of the truck. As he approached, Roth noted the tension in his shoulders and the stiffness of his gait. His steps were no less carefully placed than usual, but Nick's body was as taut as a bow string.

Once he was within a foot or two of the stairs leading up onto the porch, Nick finally spoke.

"We need to talk."

Pressing his heel into the floorboards, Roth set his chair to a gentle rock. Turning his hand palm side up, he continued to look at Nick.

"Okay. Talk."

Nick muttered, but not low enough for Roth not to hear it, which was very likely his intention. "Stubborn bastard."

"Unless they're lying, my parents were married when I was born. And if you came here to insult me some more, you can get in your truck and go back the way you came."

He knew goading Nick wasn't helpful, but Roth couldn't stop himself. Besides their normal familiarity and history of bantering, he wasn't feeling very generous at the moment. Even *knowing it was possible he was making the situation worse, he couldn't keep his mouth shut.*

Shooting him a glare, Nick pursed his lips before finally speaking again. "I didn't come here to start any shit with you, Rotty. We've been friends too long to let bullshit come between us."

"What the hell is that supposed to mean? Your bullshit or are you saying—"

"I'm not saying you and Autumn being together is bullshit. I'm talking about what's happening right now. Everything I say seems to come out wrong, or you take it in a way I didn't intend."

Nick leaned one shoulder against the post at the top of the stairs. With his arms folded across his chest, Roth stared at his friend.

"It ain't about the way I take it. It's kind of hard not to think the worst with the way you acted a few days ago. Behaving like I'm some kind of fuck boy you need to run off. Not to mention the shit you said about me paying Autumn for sex."

Holding up a hand, Nick looked at him with a clenched jaw and his version of a pleading expression.

"Can we not mention my little sister and sex in the same breath?" When Roth didn't say anything else, Nick continued. "I know I fucked up. Okay? And I apologized to Autumn for being an ass. But, have you looked at it from my view point?"

At Roth's responding shrug, Nick ventured farther onto the porch, sitting in one of the four empty rockers. Taking off his hat, he hung it on the arm of the chair.

"You've known my sister since she was a little girl. It was no secret she had a huge crush on you. Seeing you two together, having even an inkling of what happened between you, it took me to a bad headspace."

Roth refused to acknowledge the implications Nick made. If he did, he couldn't guarantee they wouldn't come to blows. He heard the question in Nick's voice. The one waiting to be asked. So, he remained silent, seeing how deep Nick would dig the hole and unsure if he'd extend a hand to help his longtime friend climb out of it.

"You told my pops you hadn't seen Autumn in years. But, I know you. Starting up with her isn't something you'd do without putting thought into it."

Roth silently acknowledged Nick had finally said something that made sense.

"If I'm to believe you two just started up, then my question is, how long?"

Knowing him so well, Nick didn't have to elaborate on his question. Roth understood. He wanted to know how long it had been since Roth had stopped looking at Autumn as just his friend's little sister and started viewing her as a woman. At this point, Roth had nothing to hide.

"The wedding."

"What wedding?"

"Hers. To the cousin fucker."

Roth refused to call Russell anything other than what he and Nick had settled on once they learned the woman Autumn caught him with was the same woman he'd claimed was his cousin.

"That was more than a decade ago." Nick shook his head in disbelief.

"I know." Roth's expression remained the same.

"Why did you wait?" Nick's posture relaxed a little, and he leaned his back into the wooden slats of the rocker.

"Why do you think?"

The look Roth shot Nick telegraphed the things they'd gone through collectively and individually during those years. They weren't together during the mission which led Roth to resign his commission. By then, they were leading separate teams.

But it wasn't only the wounds from his time serving, it was the situation they found themselves in now. The strain on their friendship because he finally acted on the desire he'd pressed down for almost fifteen years.

Silence stretched between them. Only the sounds of the ranch settling for the day could be heard. Tilting his head, Nick peered at Roth.

"I don't want to know anything about what you two do together."

"I wasn't planning to give you a play by play."

"I don't even want the Cliffsnotes."

"Again. Wasn't planning to tell you."

"My sister better keep a permanent smile on her face. But, I don't need details on how you put it there. Just know if it slips, our next talk will involve far less words."

Staring at him blankly, Roth eventually nodded. He didn't need Nick's threats. His mission was to keep Autumn so happy any thoughts she had about being anywhere other than with him, wouldn't dare to enter her mind.

"And one more thing. I don't know if she told you, but Tummy's been going through some stuff at work. Mama and Pops are already on her to come home. She doesn't need any more pressure from you."

Roth sat up straighter, he didn't like where this was going. Having Autumn return to Lone Star Ridge was definitely on the table for him.

"Promise me you'll let her decide on her own. If what the two of you have is going to go the distance, she can't relocate her life just for you. It's not fair to her. So... promise."

As thoughts swirled inside him, Roth understood the truth of what Nick said. Didn't mean he liked it, but he understood. However, he wasn't certain he could promise not to provide any incentive to help Autumn come to the right decision. Nick stared

at him expectantly. Finally, Roth dipped his chin in acknowl-
edgement.

"I won't press her." When Nick nodded, Roth held up a
hand continuing, "I won't press her, but I won't stop showing her
the benefits of being here surrounded by people who care about
her."

Present

Roth snapped out of the memory, returning his focus to
rounding up the stragglers. Now that his Sugar was home, he
was anxious to wrap things up. He'd asked Amelia to cook
Autumn's favorite meal. Miraculously, his housekeeper
complied without a single sly remark. Probably because she
really liked Autumn. Amelia commented about him being less
of a grump lately, and she attributed the attitude adjustment
to Autumn's appearance at the Lazy Creek.

He wouldn't argue the point, but he didn't give her fuel
for her little jabs. Whether it was having his Sugar in his life or
having her beside him each night chasing away the demons
from his dreams, Roth was doing more living these days. More
than he had in longer than he wanted to admit.

After he and the guys got the last of the herd where they
wanted them, he bid them goodbye. Once he'd given Big Tex a
rub down with a wet sponge, looking him over for any hitch-
hikers and small injuries, Roth set him loose in the paddock.
Noting there was plenty of water and some of the sweet grass
the horse liked to nibble on available, he turned the rest of Big
Tex's care over to the stable hand.

The short ride to the main house in his ATV, was unevent-
ful. However, a frown dipped his brow as he drove the small
vehicle toward the front porch. There was a man standing
there speaking to Autumn. The guy looked vaguely familiar,
but Roth couldn't place him immediately. When he was
within her line of sight, Autumn's face stretched into a smile.

Giving him a wave, she turned back to the man, accepting the package he held in his hands.

Now, who the fuck was this guy, and what was he giving her? Throwing the ATV into park, Roth levered himself out of it much more quickly than usual, making his way toward them to get answers.

Chapter Fourteen

Autumn smiled at Clay while shaking her head. Despite having told her Grandma Hattie not to bother, the woman had sent him over with the package they'd spoken about earlier. She really wished she hadn't bothered. Just as Clay was telling her the instructions her grandma had given him, Autumn heard the sounds of an All-Terrain Vehicle. Roth and the hands used them to get around on the ranch.

Seeing him approaching, she felt her cheeks lift with the smile taking over her face. With a short wave, she turned her attention back to the package Clay presented to her. Accepting it, Autumn tucked it under her arm, thanking him again. The words had no sooner left her lips than Roth was standing beside her slipping an arm around her waist.

The kiss he planted on her lips was accompanied by his normal greeting.

"Evenin', Sugar."

Flicking those honey-colored eyes toward Clay he looked back at her. "I didn't know we were having company."

To his credit, Clay took a step back when Roth

approached. Autumn's internal head shake spilled over into the real world as she stared up at Roth. *This man...*

"Roth, this is Clay. He works as a ranch hand at Sunset. Grandma Hattie asked him to drop off a package that came in the mail for me today."

Either oblivious or genuinely a sweet guy, Clay extended a hand to Roth.

"Nice to meet you, sir. I've met a few of your guys around town. They have nothing but good things to say about you."

While Roth accepted the handshake, his only response sounded like more of a grunt. In response, Clay cleared his throat. He looked at Autumn before quickly averting his gaze to Roth, then the floorboards between his feet.

"Well, uh. Ma'am. Like I said. Your Grandma Hattie thought you should have that sooner rather than later. I need to get back and grab a little chow before the rest of the fellas eat it all."

In a very old-fashioned move, Clay placed two fingers at the brim of his hat, tipping it toward her. Flicking a quick glance at Roth, he mumbled, "Mr. Stephens."

"Thank you again, Clay."

Autumn waved to him as he turned to leave the porch. With the package still clamped under one arm, she used the fingertips of the other hand to tap Roth's forearm. The second Clay was inside his pickup, beginning to back away from the house, she looked up at Roth.

She was quite certain the frown on her face was clear, but the indulgent look on his face said he viewed her expression as more of a pout. Narrowing her eyes, she poked him in the chest.

"There was no reason for you to be so rude to him. He was only doing what my granny asked him to do. And, he was very respectful."

Roth grabbed her fingers in one hand, bringing them to his lips then kissing them.

"I wasn't rude, Sugar. I never said a word to him."

She thought her scoffing head shake adequately conveyed her disagreement with his assessment of the situation. Rotating in his half embrace, she pulled away to enter the house.

"That's the rude part, Roth. He was polite and complimentary and you never actually spoke to him. I got the feeling he would've liked to come work for you, if you were hiring."

Walking through the door while Roth held it open for her, Autumn removed the package from beneath her arm, giving a cursory glance to the return address. Fortune Innovations, in bold typeset, was written above the physical address of their corporate offices in Las Vegas, Nevada.

"Just because I didn't show him all thirty-two of my teeth doesn't make me rude. Besides, I'm not hiring at the moment. Even if I was, I wouldn't poach anyone from Sunset."

Stopping in the foyer next to the sofa table against the right wall, Autumn gave Roth a half smile.

"That's nice of you, but I don't know that it's necessary. My dad and Uncle Clint have been talking about getting rid of the rest of the livestock and leasing larger sections of the land. None of us kids want to run a ranch, and they don't either."

Placing the unopened package on the sofa table, she faced him, loosely folding her arms across her middle.

"Honestly, they've probably only let it go this long because Grandma Hattie doesn't want to leave, and it makes her feel useful to go out checking on things and cooking the occasional meal for guys."

Standing just inside the door, Roth toed off his boots before picking them up. She'd learned during her short extended overnight stays... *Was that what she was calling what they were doing?* Anyway. Autumn noticed during her time there, if he'd been working with the hands, he usually entered the house through a mudroom where he left his boots. He only came in through the front when there was a visitor on his porch.

His dark honey gaze was trained on her while he completed his task. Looking past her to the table, he returned his eyes to hers.

"You aren't going to open that?"

A jerky head shake was Autumn's initial response.

"Why not?"

"Because I have a good idea of what it is and I'm on sabbatical. Which means, I don't do anything related to Fortune Innovations."

They'd spoken some about her return to Lone Star Ridge, but she'd only scratched the surface of her reasons for taking time off. Beyond stating she was burned out and needed a breather, there was no mention of the particulars which had brought her to that point.

Thankfully, Roth hadn't pressed. Just like she hadn't pressed him for more details surrounding his decision to leave the military. He was forthcoming whenever she asked, but Autumn didn't push. She was aware there were things he'd never be able to tell her about that time in his life. The scars on his shoulder and leg told part of the story for him, but she was certain there was much more. However, the arrival of the mystery package from Fortune had made their tacit agreement moot.

"So, being on sabbatical means you don't even open your mail? What if it's important?"

Lifting a single eyebrow, Autumn looked from Roth's confused expression to the object of their discussion atop the mahogany table.

"If it's important, they should probably consult one of the other twenty or thirty odd attorneys employed there."

While Autumn was aware she was damn good at her job, there were other competent lawyers on Fortune's payroll. Normally, she would've ripped the envelope open the second it was handed to her. Most people who knew her were aware of her penchant for getting on top of an issue and solving the problem. Which was likely why Roth was confused.

But part of what she'd been working on before she took time away from work, was setting boundaries and sticking to them. Not being in communication with anyone at Fortune regarding work was a boundary she'd clearly stated when she'd submitted her paperwork to Human Resources.

Shrugging, she looked back to see Roth had advanced farther into the house. He was much closer than he was a moment before. It was only when he was within a few inches of where she stood that he stopped. Still holding his boots in one hand, he trailed his fingertips from her shoulder down her arm before wrapping them around her wrist.

"It's not like you to avoid things, Sugar."

"I'm not avoiding anything. At worst I'm refusing to do someone else's job for them."

What she didn't say to Roth was she highly suspected the package was from Flint Childers and she didn't even know how he knew which address to use. Her personal assistant was the only one she'd shared her physical location with. And Rachel detested Flint Childers.

Squeezing her wrist, he waited until she tilted her chin upwards to drop a kiss on her lips.

"If you say so. I'm gonna go shower before dinner." Standing to his full height, one corner of his lips lifted in a sort of smile. "Wanna join me?"

Knowing what he was asking, Autumn returned his half grin with a full one.

"That's why I'm here, remember? You invited me to

dinner. Well, it was more of a demand, but we can agree to disagree on that one."

It was hard to stifle her giggle when he tightened his hold tugging her until her front was flush with his.

"You know damn well I'm not talking about dinner. You're determined to get your ass spanked aren't you?"

Wide eyes met his. "I have no idea what you're talking about, Mr. Stephens. I simply answered your question."

"Is that so?" The full octave drop in his voice should've been a clue, but Autumn kept up her routine.

"Yes. You said you were going to take a shower before dinner. The dinner you invited me to. So, I don't know why you'd ask me if I'd want to join you. It's the whole reason I'm here."

The thud of Roth's boots landing on the curved edge of the bottom step was louder than Autumn felt was completely necessary. She was powerless to control her startled jump, which put her firmly against his hard body. Placing her hands on his chest, she reared back. But, it was too late.

Roth's strong arms wrapped around her holding her against his thick frame. She was never more aware of his physical size than when he held her that way. Roth didn't so much as grunt when she suddenly leaned into him. One large hand cupped her ass while the other cradled her back between her shoulder blades.

"Is this what we're doing, Sugar? Telling fibs?"

The space between his words and when Autumn's world tilted upside down was miniscule. She couldn't definitively say he didn't squeeze her ass before tossing her over his shoulder, because it happened so quickly. The trip up the stairs was quick as she balanced herself with her arms extended and her hands pressed into his lower back.

His very firm ass was less than an inch away from her fingertips. The second they came to a complete stop, she took advantage of the proximity, giving a smack to one rounded cheek.

"That's for manhandling me."

An explanation wasn't required, but the words flew from Autumn's mouth as she delivered a firm tap to the other cheek. Couldn't have it feel left out. She should've been able to predict Roth's response, but she still yelped when her treatment of his posterior was returned. When the slap to her right ass cheek was immediately followed by one to her left, she screeched.

"Ow! No fair. Your hands are bigger than mine."

Not the best argument she could've made, but it was the one Autumn had.

"You should've thought of that before you decided to get sassy."

Setting her on her feet, Roth kept one arm around her while he reached into the shower to flick on the water. His natural scent mixed with the smell of the outdoors. Amazingly, she didn't find it unpleasant. In fact, she inhaled deeply to take it in before he washed it away.

Once the sound of water bouncing off tiles filled the room, Roth gave her his full attention again. His hand at her nape encouraged her onto her tiptoes to receive his kiss. He'd get zero objection from Autumn. She always seemed to be on a low simmer when it came to him.

Buttons were abused, and clothing stretched and ripped in their haste to get undressed. It was as if turning on the water had been tantamount to opening the gate allowing the bucking bull and rider to enter the arena. Limbs flailed, grasped and groped in an effort to reveal skin to join them together.

In a matter of seconds, they were inside the shower with her back pressed against the wall as Roth held her up, impaling her on his thickness. Sparring via text had started their foreplay. They picked it up in the foyer. So, very little preparation was needed for her to be ready to receive him.

"Fuck, Sugar. You're so hot. So tight. You take my cock like you were made for it."

"Roth!"

Autumn was consumed with desire. His name was the only word she could push past her lips. He filled her so completely she was a massive bundle of nerves—simply feeling. When he angled them so that he could take her nipple into his mouth, she nearly came undone. Combining breast play with the precision strokes he delivered to her pussy was too much.

She lasted longer than the storied eight seconds of a bull rider, but it was safe to say they'd both won this round. As Autumn's body went rigid, her channel undulated around Roth's dick coating it in her essence. Her screams bounced off the tiled walls before he swallowed them with his kisses, feeding her his responding groans.

Soon after her climax, Roth joined her in bliss. With one final, firm thrust, he buried himself inside her to the hilt, releasing his seed. His grinding movement at the location where they were joined, rubbed Autumn's clit just right, triggering a second orgasm.

"Fuck, Roth!"

"That's it, Sugar. Give it all to me."

Roth's encouragements were the last words to reach Autumn through a haze. The second climax was so powerful, she nearly passed out. Holding on to consciousness by a thread, she watched him from half lowered lids. Placing her on the built-in bench on the far end of the shower, he cleaned himself before returning to perform the same for her. Eventually, they made it downstairs to eat the dinner he'd invited her to share with him.

Chapter Fifteen

Roth looked down at the phone in his hand. A text message notification had come in just as he'd ended a call with Ryker. His brother was checking to make sure he was still going to stop by the tailor to get his measurements taken.

The actual tuxedos were being made by a haberdasher in Las Vegas. A place called Savile. His brother being his brother, he wouldn't accept the measurements Roth rattled off as accurate, he wanted a professional to take them. So, he'd made arrangements with someone in Houston.

It was a good thing Roth was already planning to be in the city to handle some business. He'd groused about potentially making a special trip just to have his legs measured, but he would've done it. If for no other reason than to keep his brother from worrying about something so small being handled.

He was actively walking through the nondescript shopping complex when Ryker called. Their conversation was quick, but Roth stopped to read the message he'd received from his Sugar.

> I won't be over tonight. I'm going to stay
> with Granny. We're cooking dinner and
> having a girls' night.

Frowning at the screen, Roth bit the inside of his lip. *Here she goes with this shit again.* They were both well aware that she didn't **come over** as much as she was always there. Most of the clothes she'd brought with her were at the Lazy Creek. She'd have to pack a bag to spend the night at her Grandma Hattie's. Not the other way around.

However, she didn't want to admit she was essentially living with him. It wasn't a secret where she'd spent the majority of the last three months. With him. In his bed. Waking beside him each morning.

> When will you be home?

Propping against the wall a few stores away from the place Ryker made the appointment, Roth watched the cellphone screen as the notification bubbles appeared, disappeared, then reappeared before Autumn's next message came over.

> I'll see you tomorrow. I may have breakfast
> with Granny, then I have a meeting at the
> Daley Group. I'll come over when I'm done.

Roth's gut tightened. They'd parted ways earlier when she'd left to follow up with someone about an issue she'd been working on for the company. That was hours ago. Now she was saying he wouldn't see her again for possibly another twenty-four hours? Nope. That wasn't gonna happen.

> If you don't think you can make it home for
> breakfast in the morning, I'll come by Miss
> Hattie's before I check in with the guys.

Roth...

> Gotta go. I'm about to be late for my
> appointment.

Slipping the phone into this back pocket, Roth grinned to himself. *Two can play that game, Sugar.* He knew he was pushing her buttons with his insistence on calling the Lazy Creek their home. But, that's because it was. She just needed to come to grips with it.

Once he was done imitating a mannequin in the tailor's shop, Roth had a thought. Looking around, he located a visual display which included a map of the shopping area. Finding the place he needed, he set off in the direction of the custom scent shop.

Just as he drew near the store featuring the two interlocked letter Es representing the shop's name, Essence Envy, Roth noticed movement in his periphery. It was a public place, so people being nearby wasn't unexpected, but intuition prodded him to look to his left.

Initially, the couple didn't look familiar. However, when the man turned, Roth saw his full face. Years had passed, but he was nearly certain he was looking at Autumn's former fiancé.

Roth's suspicion was confirmed when the woman he was with said the man's name.

"Russell. Russell!" Jerking back around, the cousin fucker looked at the woman with wide eyes before his expression settled into a frown.

"What?"

"I want to go in here."

"For what?"

"It's a clothing store." The woman responded dryly. "To look at clothes."

Roth didn't catch Russell's response and didn't really care. He'd reached his destination. Ducking to miss the bell tinkling above the door, Roth stepped into Essence Envy without looking back.

"Good afternoon, sir. Welcome to Essence Envy. Can I help you create something?"

The cheerful greeting and offer came from a pretty woman with a dark bronze complexion. Her hair framed her face in waves making her look like she should be on an advertisement for a tropical vacation.

"Yes, ma'am. You can. I'd like to get a few things made, but I'm not sure where to start."

"Call me, Julia."

Her smile broadened as she waved him over to a counter containing small bottles filled with liquids ranging in color from clear to dark brown. Once they were there, she began asking questions. After they'd established he wasn't looking for anything for himself, the queries became more specific.

Roth was on the verge of regretting his bright idea by the time he set the small cup of coffee grounds onto the counter to sniff the latest fragrance she presented to him. As he waved the scent stick under his nose, he listened as she described the scent and the notes it would add to the overall fragrance they were crafting.

Nodding in agreement, Roth passed it back. They had just finished discussing the particular products when the bell above the door tinkled announcing a new customer.

"Hello. Welcome to Essence Envy. Feel free to look around, I'll be with you in just a moment."

Glancing over his shoulder, Roth saw the cousin fucker and the woman from earlier. While the woman immediately began wandering around to the different displays, he hung back. Enough time had passed for Roth's anger at the way Russell hurt Autumn to dim. So, the urge to kick his ass again wasn't as strong. But his disdain for the shit stain remained solid. Which meant the option wasn't completely off the table.

"Okay, Mr. Stephens, I can have everything ready for you by tomorrow afternoon. However, if you're willing to wait for twenty to thirty minutes, you can take the perfume with you today."

Roth looked at his watch. He had the time. The problem was, even when he was a teenager, hanging out at the mall had never been his thing. Loitering around the store wasn't looking like a viable choice either. He didn't give two shits about the woman and her unfaithful companion, but Roth couldn't one hundred percent trust himself if Russell made the mistake of speaking to him. In the few seconds of his hesitation, Julia spoke again.

"I promise it won't be longer than that. Our other perfumer is due back any moment. So, I'll be able to give it my undivided attention. You can also watch the process."

As if Julia conjured her, the door behind the counter opened and another woman walked through.

"Right on cue. Should I get to work on the perfume, Mr. Stephens?"

Seeing the other perfumer approach the couple to engage them, Roth nodded. Taking a seat on one of the stools in front of the mixing station, he settled in to wait. Watching Julia take the scented oils he selected, measure them out, and begin the blending process was actually very interesting.

While he was conscious of the others in the store, he was able to regulate their presence to an awareness only level. That is until he detected elevated voices with an angry undercurrent. Swiveling on the stool, he regarded the couple. Their voices weren't loud, but his situational awareness training hadn't dulled simply because he left the military.

The other perfumer's back was to the couple and the

woman was glaring at Russell. His expression projected a mix of defiance and annoyance.

"Are you seriously doing this right in my face?"

"Doing what, Lucy? Being polite to the person helping you spend my money?"

"Don't play crazy with me. I'm not stupid."

Brushing her off, Russell looked away. When his gaze landed on Roth, there was no attempt on Roth's part to pretend he wasn't listening to the exchange. From the rings on their fingers and the content of the conversation, it sounded as if the cousin fucker and his pretend cousin, Lucy, were still together.

If Roth hazarded a guess, he'd been as faithful to her as he'd been to Autumn. Not a surprise. He'd seen it too many times to count with members of his unit and soldiers on post. Cheaters didn't stop cheating simply because one partner wouldn't put up with their shit. And the woman they cheated *with* simply became the next woman they cheated *on*.

Apparently, Russell's attempt to ignore Lucy only served to make her angrier.

"Are you fucking her too?"

"What?! Are you serious? I don't even know this woman. I only came in this damn store because you've begged me to spend some time with you. I do what you want, and you start shit with me for being polite. I can't fucking win."

Stomping away from her, Russell beat a path to the door while Lucy trailed after him. She was immediately contrite and apologetic, but the asshole never stopped walking. Shaking his head, Roth didn't turn back toward Julia until they were gone.

Julia was a woman of her word. In less than thirty minutes, she presented him with a package prettily wrapped in lavender and pink paper with a bow affixed to the top. She placed it inside a bag with the store logo on the front. Paying for the item and the remainder of his order, Roth thanked her before leaving.

He'd completely put the interaction he'd observed between Lucy and Russell out of his mind. His thoughts had already turned to his plans for the remainder of the evening. There was one more stop he needed to make before heading back to the ranch. A grin tilted his lips as he thought about it.

"I suppose that was funny to you."

Bitter words laced with tears came to Roth from a bench to his left. Not breaking stride, he didn't bother to look at or acknowledge Lucy. There was no reason to. They'd never been more than passing acquaintances all those years ago. He owed her nothing.

The quick tapping of her footfalls on the pavement told him his lack of response wasn't going to deter her. With a heaving sigh, he stopped. Piercing her with an aggravated expression, Roth already knew he'd regret even speaking to her.

"Lady, I don't know, nor do I care to know you. So, no. I don't find anything funny, since I wasn't even thinking about either of you."

Having said his piece, Roth resumed his trek to his truck. When the taps against the concrete continued to follow him, he stopped again. His arms remained at his side with the small bag looped onto two fingers on his left hand.

"What do you want?" Roth had neither the time nor inclination to play nice.

"I know who you are."

"So do I. What's your point?"

"I know people in Lone Star Ridge. They told me you and Autumn are a thing now."

"What the fuck does that have to do with you?"

Roth's scowl deepened. This conversation was pointless,

but his gut said the only way to keep her from following him to his truck was to get it over with.

Instead of answering his question, she continued to ramble. "They told me you bought her in a charity auction. That you dropped a hundred thousand dollars on her."

Her face could've been pretty, if it wasn't filled with such bitterness and obvious jealousy.

"What do y'all see in her? She's not worth all that effort."

Roth didn't owe her an explanation, but he wouldn't allow her to talk bad about Autumn in his presence.

"Look, lady. And I use that word loosely. I don't owe you or anyone else an explanation for what I do with my money. But as for Autumn Daley, what she's worth can't be measured in currency. If you can't see it, that's a you problem.

You're jealous and bitter. Again, a you problem. But it's in your best interest to swallow that shit and pretend you never met her. Whatever is going on with you and the cheating shit stain you married has nothing to do with me and Autumn."

Dismissing her, he continued to his vehicle. When he'd made it two steps, he heard the tip-tap of steps coming closer. Whirling on her, he gave her the full force of his glare.

"Stop fucking following me." The low, near growl was laced with his frustration. *What the fuck was this woman's damage?* "I'm not your minister, your priest or your counselor. Find someone else to work out your issues with."

"But why? Why do y'all keep choosing her?"

Roth stared at the woman in disbelief. Tears gathered in her eyes and spilled down her cheeks. He wasn't heartless, but he couldn't drum up an ounce of sympathy for her.

What the hell did she expect him to do? Shaking his head, Roth walked away. Long strides made it such that she'd have to run to keep up with him. Soon, she stopped trying.

Chapter Sixteen

Autumn stood in the doorway leading into the family room staring at the scene inside. After she'd told Roth she was staying at Grandma Hattie's for the night, she should've been suspicious of how quickly he acquiesced. Other than him insisting on calling his ranch her home, he hadn't put up even a slight argument. That should've been a huge, blazing, red flag. But she didn't see it.

So, imagine her surprise when she was elbow deep in biscuit dough and he sauntered in with a box and a small bag in his hands. Her grandma didn't have her back in the least, inviting Roth inside while eyeing the distinctly shaped box he carried.

Without even looking inside, Autumn knew it was a hat from the clothing store/hat shop most of the older, church going, African American women in the area relied on for their first Sunday hats and attire. Imagining Roth walking into the store and perusing the hats brought a reluctant smile to Autumn's face since she knew it would probably be talked about amongst the ladies for a good long while.

Squealing and giggling like a teenager, Grandma Hattie

lifted the shimmering pearl colored hat from the box. She immediately went to the mirror in the hallway to try it on, tugging at the stiff organza to arrange it just so to cover one eye. The entire time she talked about how jealous the other church mothers were going to be when they saw it.

The hat was Roth's get out of jail free card. She couldn't be upset when he'd made her grandma so happy. Approaching her at the island, he set the small bag just beyond where she had the dough rolled. Standing next to her, he slid an arm around her waist before pressing a kiss to her cheek.

"Evenin', Sugar. I brought you a little somethin'."

Slanting him a glance, Autumn pursed her lips. He was pouring on the country charm. And, it was working. Although she'd never considered receiving gifts to be one of the ways she measured affection, it was nice that he'd bought her something simply because he wanted her to have it. The cherry on top was him being considerate by including her grandmother.

Now, he was relaxed in the corner of the sectional in the family room flipping through the options, patiently waiting for her grandma to choose the movie she wanted to watch.

"Little girl, are you gonna just stand there, or can I have my popcorn?"

"Sorry, Granny. Here you go."

Passing her grandmother the bowl containing the mixture of salted caramel and white cheddar popcorn, Autumn placed the other bowl on the coffee table within Roth's reach. When she went to step away, she suddenly found herself tilting backwards. Landing with a light oomph against Roth's hard body, Autumn shot him a censuring glance.

"Roth!" Her gaze shot to her grandmother, who was staring at the television, eating her popcorn, and studiously ignoring them.

"Don't mind me. You sitting cuddled up next to Child is probably the tamest stuff the two of you get up to."

"Granny!" Autumn's jaw hung in shock.

"What? I'm old, not dead. I was young once. If I told you a quarter of the things me and your grandfather got up to, it would turn your hair white."

Autumn's hands shot to her ears. "La-la-la-la-la. I can't hear you."

Her grandmother's cackling laughter preceded the popcorn she tossed at her.

"I said, if I told you. I'm not actually going to do it. I don't kiss and tell."

Autumn's shoulders slumped in relief. "Thank God."

Her remark garnered her another few kernels of cheesy popcorn being tossed in her direction.

"Granny!"

"Stop being a smartie pants." Laughter coated her grandmother's words and Autumn joined in. She felt Roth's chuckles against her back. "Child, let's watch that one. The ladies said that handsome young man with the pretty eyes was kickin' ass and taking names."

"Yes, ma'am."

Autumn shook her head as Roth dutifully started the recently released movie about a former soldier fighting corrupt cops in a small town. As excited as she'd sounded when she'd made her selection, her grandmother was asleep less than halfway through the movie. By that point, both Autumn and Roth were invested.

Suspending her disbelief, Autumn refrained from pointing out the legal aspects which weren't quite accurate. But, seeing as she practiced corporate law, it wasn't to say she was totally correct. Roth only grunted and grumbled a couple of times about things he disagreed with. Mostly, it was minute details only someone with his specialized training would notice.

As the credits were rolling, they began clearing away the remnants of their movie snacks. With a hand to her shoulder, Autumn gently jostled her grandmother.

"Granny? The movie's over."

"It's over?" With the cutest look of confusion on her face, Autumn's grandma stared at her with sleep fogged eyes.

"Yes, ma'am. It's over. Do you need help getting ready for bed?"

"I'm not a baby, Autumn Marianne. I know how to wash my face and put on a nightgown."

"Yes, ma'am."

Autumn was just relieved to hear she had no plans to attempt to shower or get into a bathtub. In her current state of drowsiness, Autumn worried she'd slip and fall. After she watched her grandmother walk down the hallway and enter her bedroom, Autumn followed the sound of running water into the kitchen.

Roth stood at the sink, washing the bowls and glasses they'd used for their popcorn and drinks. For a moment, she hovered in the doorway watching the play of muscles in his back as he performed the mundane task.

"If you're just gonna stand there ogling me, at least get out some singles."

"Singles?" Autumn stepped closer, not stopping until she could wrap her arms around his waist. "You've got to know I wouldn't wave around anything smaller than a hunny. Not for you."

Roth's glance over his shoulder held a lopsided grin. "A hunny? Where'd you get that from, Sugar?"

"That's not what they say? I have a pocket full of hunnies." Autumn bobbed her head to a beat only she could hear.

Placing the last glass onto the drying rack, Roth used the towel to dry his hands. Turning, he looped both arms around her, holding her close.

"I'm not up on all the current slang, but I think they still call one-hundred-dollar bills, c-notes or Benjamins. I recall a few of the fellas refer to them as Big Head Bens. What I haven't heard a soul call them, is hunnies."

"Maybe you need to get out more." Autumn brushed her fingers along the soft material of the t-shirt covering his impressive chest.

"I get out plenty. And if what I experienced today is any indicator, I've been right to spend most of my time at the ranch."

"What happened today?" Autumn's brow dipped. But before Roth could answer, she rose on her tiptoes to give him a quick peck on the lips. "Thank you again for my perfume."

"You're welcome, Sugar." Guiding her away from the sink, he wrapped an arm around her waist. "Let's go out on the porch, and I'll tell you about it."

"Okay."

Autumn didn't resist his guiding hand. It was a relatively cool night and her grandma's porch was screened in. So, she wouldn't have to fight off too many mosquitos to enjoy sitting outside.

Once they were settled on the lounging seat, Roth told her about his visit to the shopping center, then running into Russell and Lucy. She wasn't exactly ecstatic to hear about him seeing her former fiancé, but she really couldn't muster up enough give a fuck to care.

Hearing that Lucy thought Russell was up to his cheating ways didn't surprise her. What did Lucy expect considering how the two began their relationship? What was more surprising was that she was still hanging on. Autumn would bet a month's salary Russell's philandering wasn't a new development.

However, when Roth mentioned Lucy's little rant after he stepped out of the fragrance shop, Autumn shot up from her position leaning against his chest.

"What the fuck is wrong with her? Who in their right minds thinks it's okay to do stuff like that?"

Although she allowed Roth to tuck her back into his side while he ran his big, warm, hands up and down her back, Autumn was seething. *That bitch!*

"I don't know, Sugar. Honestly, I'm not sure I wanna know. But something she said got me thinking."

Tilting her head, Autumn looked up to find him staring at her. Without thought, her fingers splayed on his chest, rubbing in light circles.

"Got you thinking about what? What did she say?"

"She asked why we **kept** choosing you over her. Since I don't really know her from a cow patty, I'm guessing she's actually talking about her shit stain husband.

I know what happened to make you call off your wedding is a sensitive subject. But her question doesn't make sense considering he married her. Why would she say he kept choosing you over her?"

Averting her eyes, Autumn shrugged and snuggled back into his side. She hoped her non-verbal response was enough for him because she'd been Russell free for a while. She didn't want the toxic bullshit between him and his fake cousin to affect her relationship with Roth.

"Don't do that, Sugar. I'm a quick study, and I've learned your tells. What haven't you told me?"

Normally, the gruff quality in his voice would skate over her skin, making her want to climb him and press her body as close to him as humanly possible. This time, the censure in his tone made her want to burrow beneath his arm to keep from confronting his perceptiveness. Using one thick finger, he lifted her chin until she was forced to look at him.

"What have you been hiding, Sugar?"

"Nothing!" Realizing her immediate response came out much sharper than she intended, Autumn tried again. "I'm not hiding anything."

Roth's honey colored gaze probed hers for a moment before he spoke again. "Let me rephrase. What has been happening that you didn't think was worth mentioning?"

He should've been a fucking lawyer. He'd made it impossible for her to answer any other way but honestly. She didn't appreciate him sussing out the correct method of extracting the information seeing as she didn't consider the incidents worthy of discussion.

"Technically, I haven't seen Russell, in person, since the day I called off the wedding. I cut off all contact with him and any mutual friends that we had. Because fuck them. I felt like they knew that bitch wasn't really his cousin.

Anyway, a few months after I settled into law school, I got a message on social media. Once I realized it was Russell, I blocked him. He didn't have my phone number, because I changed it and only close family and friends had it.

I never entertained any of the messages he sent, except for once. He said he knew where I was, and if I didn't respond, he would come to me."

"Sugar?! Why the fuck didn't you tell someone?" Autumn flinched at the anger and roughness in Roth's voice. But, his hold on her was gentle, in direct contrast to his tone.

"There was nothing to tell, Roth. I handled it. I reminded him of the ass whooping you and Nick gave him. I told him, if he didn't want a repeat performance, he should forget he knew me."

Roth stared at her for a beat, and before he spoke, Autumn heard it coming.

"What else?"

Chapter Seventeen

Roth couldn't believe Autumn had been hiding the fact that Russell had been harassing her all this time. His gut said there was more to it than the annoying messages she mentioned. He had half a mind to drive back to Houston and give the piece of shit a refresher course on why it was a bad idea for him to even speak Autumn's name.

"What else, Sugar? Russell didn't seem like the kind of guy who responded well to words alone."

When her bottom lip fell victim to her teeth, Roth knew she was still holding back. He was well aware she wasn't doing it to protect Russell. She was worried about what Roth, Nick or both would do in response. Because, there was no way in hell he wasn't gonna tell Nick about that motherfucker ignoring their warning.

Of course, Roth would make certain the message was crystal clear. Then, Nick could have what was left—if there was anything left. Finally, Autumn's teeth released their captive.

"It's nothing. And like I said I handled it."

"Sugar..."

The warning in the single word changed the endearment. Roth didn't miss the widening of her eyes before resolve caused her shoulders to slump slightly.

"I was at a legal conference. I can't say for certain he orchestrated being at the same conference, but I saw him there. It was last year. Since I hadn't heard from him in so long, I figured he'd finally gotten the message.

After one of the sessions, he approached me asking if we could have drinks and catch up. I looked at him like he'd lost his mind and declined. When he grabbed my arm, I put him on his ass. Someone called security. Once I explained what happened, they escorted him away and I never saw him again."

"So, you just lied to me. You said you hadn't seen him in person since the wedding."

Roth felt Autumn's body go rigid. Her thoughts may as well have been scrolling across her forehead like a news ticker. She'd somehow forgotten what she said when he admitted to having a run in with Russell.

"I – uh." Roth remained quiet, watching as she stumbled before composing herself enough to speak again.

"I didn't intentionally lie."

"So, it was an accident for you to say you hadn't seen him in more than a decade when you actually saw him a year ago?"

"Roth...I wasn't thinking about the conference when I said that. I only interacted with him for those few brief minutes, and I never saw him again."

Clamping down on his hold when she attempted to shift away from him, Roth's brow creased.

"Sugar, I don't like the idea that you feel as if you have to lie to me, or omit things. Him continuing to contact you after all these years is more than the nuisance you're treating it as. The shit is weird, and it's gonna stop."

Autumn's eyes narrowed. "See. That's why I handled it

myself. Based on what happened at the wedding, I knew you and Nick would take things too far."

"There's no such thing as too far when it comes to you, Sugar."

"Roth... I'm not some damsel in distress who needs to be rescued. Russell is a non-factor in my life. I ignore him because nothing he says or does matters to me."

Moving one hand from her back to the base of her neck, Roth tangled his fingers in the hair at her nape. Keeping her face tilted upwards, he pierced her with a stare.

"See, the difference between your thinking and mine is this, it doesn't matter if you think you need saving. I'm going to protect you. And he may not mean shit to you, but you obviously matter to him.

Apparently, he's one of those guys who can't take a hint and needs to have it spelled out using a language he understands. I'm just gonna make sure he learns his lesson better this time."

Autumn's attempt to shake her head was thwarted by Roth's hold on her hair.

"Roth, you can't keep beating up people for hurting my feelings. Besides, Russell doesn't have the power to hurt me anymore. I no longer believe myself to be in love with him."

"It's good to hear you confirm you aren't in love with him, Sugar. That would definitely put a kink in our relationship. But, I didn't need to hear you say it. I already knew. There's no way you could be in love with that idiot when you're in love with me."

Autumn's gasp was accompanied by the widening of her eyes. Roth was certain his hold kept her from moving her head, but her gaze skittered away from his. Squeezing her soft curves against his hardness, Roth leaned closer to her face, forcing her to look at him again.

"No need to be shy now, baby. It's not like you're the only one feelin' it."

When he'd begun this conversation, Roth hadn't intended for it to take this turn. However, he wouldn't back away from it now. He was in love with Autumn Daley, and he knew she felt the same about him. Announcing her feelings on her behalf, before he expressed his own may not have been the most graceful way to do it, but it was done now.

"What—?" Autumn cleared her throat when the word came out as a scratchy whisper. "What does that mean? I'm not the only one feeling it?"

It was good she didn't deny loving him. Roth couldn't say how he would've responded if she'd tried to lie to him again and deny it. Caressing her jawline with his thumb, gave her a chaste kiss.

"You know what it means, Sugar. I love you. I'm *in* love with you."

Her fingertips pressing into his chest slightly stung from her rounded nails digging into him through his shirt, but Roth didn't care. He held her gaze as he watched the effect of his declaration take root.

"You love me?"

Not liking the note of disbelief in her voice, Roth lifted her onto his lap with her legs straddling his hips. Cupping her face in his hands, he kissed her again. More thoroughly this time. Her tongue met his eagerly as he attempted to show her in deed to match his words. Once he was finally able to pull back, he peered into her eyes.

"Yeah, Sugar. I love you. And if we weren't on your granny's porch, I'd show you just how much."

Autumn's crestfallen expression would've been comical if it weren't for the pressure from his cock. The greedy bastard was protesting being so close to her sweet heat without being inside. Flexing his fingers against the rounded curve of her ass, he couldn't resist giving it a squeeze.

"We don't have to be."

The frown creasing his brow had a different meaning. Roth tilted his head to one side assessingly.

"We don't have to be what?"

"On my granny's porch."

Gripping her ass, Roth shifted her against his hardness unable to stop himself from adding to his torture. Regret shook his head while he shut his eyes against her beguiling expression.

"No matter how progressive Miss Hattie is, I'm not fucking you in your grandma's house."

Increasing his torment, Autumn wound her hips rubbing her covered mons against his rapidly hardening cock.

"I wasn't asking you to. But you have a perfectly good truck parked in the driveway and a big ass bed at the Lazy Creek that we can make use of as loudly and often as we want."

"Oh yeah?" Giving in to his urge to at least put his lips on her, Roth nuzzled the crook of her neck nibbling at the exposed skin of her collarbone.

"Mhmm." Autumn's response was more of a moan. Her hands glided up his chest and around his neck. Her fingernails scraped against his scalp before she latched onto what she could manage to grab of his close-cropped hair.

"Didn't you tell your grandma you were staying the night with her?"

Roth threw it out there, but he was praying she didn't take bait and decide to stay. Her reply was the grinding wind of her hips. Gripping her jean covered ass, Roth locked down her movements.

"Fuck, Sugar. I'll go grab your bag while you leave your granny a note."

Standing with her in his arms, he stalked toward the door. Her legs wrapped around his waist and she returned the favor of raining kisses along the column of his neck. At the foot of the stairs, he reluctantly set her on her feet. Getting her moving with a tap to her sweet ass, he took the stairs two at a time to reach the bedroom she used.

The bag was easy to spot as she'd left it in the chair next to the night stand, which also held her purse. Grabbing them both, he left the room. By the time he made it downstairs, Autumn was folding a piece of paper and scribbling something on the outside of it.

That had to be the shortest note ever. Not questioning it, he waited impatiently for her to take it into the kitchen and leave it where her grandmother was sure to find it. In less than five minutes, they were in his truck speeding down the road. Not for the first time, he wished there was more than a horse trail connecting the two properties. If there was, he was certain he could cut the time it took them to get home in half.

They still made exceptional time. Roth barely had them through the door before they were tugging at one another's clothing. He was undeterred by the ripping sound when he attacked her pants and underwear. By then, Roth knew they'd likely not make it to the bed for the first round. Taking a sharp right, he guided her into the living room, not stopping until they hit the back of the sofa.

"Turn around, Sugar."

Issuing the instruction, Roth didn't wait for compliance. Instead, he whirled Autumn around. Dropping to his knees behind her, he licked his lips as he stared at the cheeks of her high, rounded ass. Placing a hand at the center of her back, he applied pressure.

"Put your hands on the couch and hold on."

The command hit the air a millisecond before he leaned

forward and swiped his tongue along her lower lips. Inhaling deeply, he savored the aroma of her arousal.

"Fuck. You smell delicious, baby."

With two hands full of her luscious posterior, Roth delved his tongue between her labia, lapping at her leaking channel before latching onto her clit. Suckling the little bundle of nerves, he alternately caressed and delivered light smacks to her ass. With each tap, Autumn gave a little jump causing him to growl and pull her sweetness back toward him.

"Now, be a good girl and give me my prize."

Sliding two fingers into her channel, he began a dual assault stimulating her inside and out. Roth's wait for his prize was short. A few more flicks and suckles were delivered, then Autumn's keening wail hit the air. Her walls clamped around his questing digits, and he released her little bean to transfer his attention to lapping up his reward.

He didn't stop until she was draped limply over the back of the couch. Her legs trembled in their effort to support her. Reverently kissing her sweet spot, Roth stood. Raining kisses on her ass, then her back before swiping her hair to the side and tenderly pecking her neck, he admired her post orgasmic beauty.

Roth's voice was only slightly louder than a whisper when he spoke directly into her ear. The additional gruffness was evident.

"I hope you don't think I'm done with you."

"Mmm..."

Autumn's languid response made his lips curl in a smile.

"Are you ready for me, Sugar? Can you handle more?"

Despite the limpness of her repose, Autumn's nod was enthusiastic.

"Use your big girl words. Tell me."

Her response was as strained as her attempt to get her arms beneath her to push upward from the soft cushions.

"Please, Roth."

"Please what, baby?"

Rubbing the plum shaped tip of his cock along her pussy, he teased her with a shallow dip into her channel. He sent up a prayer of thanks when she put them both out of their misery.

"Please give it to me. I'm so ready."

In a sudden burst of energy, Autumn rocked her hips back, impaling herself on his hard stiffness. Gripping her ass, he tried to hold her in place. But his own body wasn't respecting his commands. His pelvic thrust buried more than half his length inside her before he regained control.

"Naughty little sugar lump. You must want me to fuck you hard. Make it so you can't walk tomorrow."

It was probably good her face was pressed into the cushions, because the look on his was likely unhinged. Taking the winding of her hips as a challenge, Roth flexed his fingers against her plush cheeks pulling her into each of his strokes.

He had to close his eyes against the erotic vision of his cock disappearing into her honeyed depths. Seeing it while feeling her heat engulf his entire shaft was enough to make him blow his load within seconds. His woman deserved better than that. And he gave it to her. Roth didn't offer either of them relief until her walls fluttered around his thickness and her wails became hoarse screams announcing her climax.

"That's it, Sugar. Milk my cock. Take it. Take all of me."

Murmuring encouragement into her ear, Roth's entire body stiffened as he released his seed. It was much longer than he'd anticipated before they were able to make it upstairs for the evening. But, he wouldn't complain about a second of it.

Chapter Eighteen

Autumn snapped the lid closed on the laptop and smiled at the woman sitting across from her.

"I say we count this as a win." The apples of her cheeks lifted higher when Floria Martinez gifted her with a broad smile of her own.

"Thank you so much, Senōra Daley."

Waving a hand, Autumn gave her a mock frown. "I told you before, my mother is Mrs. Daley. I'm Autumn. And, you're very welcome. I'm happy we were able to get things resolved so you and your husband have one less thing to worry about."

"Thank you again... Autumn." The woman spoke Autumn's name tentatively as if it tasted foreign on her tongue.

"You're welcome. I'll submit this final paperwork before I leave today." Standing, Autumn moved toward the door to escort Floria out. "Remember, if you haven't received the funds by Friday, give me a call and I'll get on the phone with them."

"Si. I mean. Yes. I understand."

Stopping at the desk of the assistant she was sharing with a few of the other executives, Autumn gave the young woman a few instructions before walking back into her office. She'd stopped thinking of the space as temporary since she'd decided to officially turn her sabbatical into a resignation from Fortune Innovations. She hadn't told them yet.

Part of her professionalism wouldn't allow her to simply send them an email. She was planning a trip to Las Vegas in a few weeks. So, her intentions were to schedule a meeting with her department head and human resources while she was there.

It would be the only potential sour part of her trip since her primary purpose was to attend Ensley and Ryker's wedding. She wasn't a member of the wedding party, and that was fine with her. They'd expressed their desire to keep things small and Ensley had her siblings, along with her best friend rounding out her bridal party. Considering what Roth said about his mother and her penchant for doing it big, Autumn was surprised, but happy the couple was getting the wedding they wanted.

Officially, Autumn was attending as Roth's plus one—although she had her own invitation to the event. She had to be his plus one, because he was finally calling in the 'date' he'd won at the charity auction. It was amusing considering it was going on close to four months of them essentially living together, and they'd said those three special words to each other.

"Ready to go, Sugar?"

Startled by the sudden question, Autumn gasped, pressing a hand to her chest. Roth stood just inside the door of her office wearing a pair of sinfully fitted jeans and a red and black plaid shirt. Her gaze raked over him appreciatively as she stood.

"Yeah. I'm all done for the day."

Sliding her laptop into her bag, she stepped around the desk and into his waiting arms. As much as she wished for more, Roth placed a chaste kiss on her lips before relieving her of the bag, slinging it onto his shoulder. Warmth radiated from her lower back where his hand was placed, and Autumn had to remind her honey pot that The Daley Group wasn't an appropriate location to initiate play time.

When they stepped outside the main doors of the building, bright sunlight caused Autumn to squint and wish she hadn't left her sunglasses in Roth's truck earlier. At least she could put them on once they reached his vehicle. They were a few steps away from the front of his Dually when a tortured voice, filled with venom reached her ears.

"Why couldn't you just stay away? You mess up everything."

Frowning, Autumn looked around to see a haggard looking... Lucy? Was that Lucy? The woman Russell claimed was his cousin only to later marry. Staring at her, Autumn didn't bother to answer. Roth's fingers flexed against her back reminding her of their destination.

"Don't engage, Sugar. She's like a tick. If you let her attach herself, she won't stop."

"I know you hear me. Why couldn't you just stay away? The minute you showed up everything went to shit."

Despite Roth's sage advice, Autumn stopped, turning fully toward Lucy. She almost felt sorry for her, but the hatred in Lucy's expression didn't lend itself to stimulating Autumn's empathy.

"Where I go is none of your business. I don't have anything to do with you or your life. If it's not working out like you planned, that sounds like a you problem."

"Don't pretend you don't know what you did. Having Russell run behind you. Comparing everyone to you...Now, you've been back here five minutes and he's been fired from his job. We can't afford our kid's tuition. But even if he had a job, he wouldn't be able to work because someone—"

Her eyes darted to Roth before returning to Autumn. "*Someone* broke his fingers and one of his arms. His jaw is still wired shut. So, he can't eat solid food."

Autumn refused to give Lucy the satisfaction of seeing even a hint of surprise on her face. She and Roth would discuss Lucy's allegations when they were alone. In the meantime, she gave Lucy the exact amount of attention she deserved.

"Lucy, like I said. This sounds like a you problem. I don't think about you or Russell. If the two of you are having a hard time, maybe you're simply reaping what you put out in the world."

Not that Roth needed her to defend him, but Autumn moved to stand directly in front of him. Folding her arms across her middle, she purposely looked down her nose at the shorter Lucy.

"I don't care for you implying that my man had something to do with Russell's condition. We both know he can't keep his dick in his pants. So, maybe you should figure out whose wife he's screwing around with to find out what happened to him."

Taking a step closer, she did something she rarely did. Autumn used her size to intimidate a smaller person. Her facial expression was hard and emotionless.

"One last thing, Luce... If you don't want to share a hospital room with your husband, perusing the liquid diet menu, let this be your last *visit*."

When Lucy looked like she was going to say something else, Autumn dropped her arms to her sides, lifting a single eyebrow as she stared at the shorter woman. Her expression was more of a promise than a dare

Once she was satisfied her message had been received,

Autumn looked over her shoulder at Roth. "I'm ready to go when you are, baby."

Casting a disgusted glance in Lucy's direction, she took Roth's hand and let him lead her to the passenger side of the truck. The entire time, Lucy stood on the sidewalk glaring. As Roth assisted her into the vehicle, building security approached Lucy encouraging her to move along. Autumn was certain someone had alerted them to the potential altercation, but she couldn't muster any sympathy for Lucy's plight.

For a couple of miles, the only sound in the cab of the truck was low music playing. Roth still had the station set to the classic R&B channel she'd changed it to earlier. Knowing he preferred nineties rock and was catering to her likes, didn't soften her thoughts following their encounter with Lucy.

As delusional and foolish over Russell as she was, Autumn was positive Lucy's assessment of who beat his ass was accurate. When Lucy mentioned it, Autumn's mind immediately went to the conversation she and Roth had about Russell not getting the message that she wanted nothing to do with him.

"Is there something you want to tell me, Roth?"

"Do I wanna tell you? No. Will I?..." Silence stretched between them for a beat before he answered his own question. "Sure, Sugar."

Even if she didn't like his delivery, or the idea that if Lucy hadn't been distraught enough to confront them, he may have never told her, Autumn had a modicum of respect for him not lying when she asked him directly. Shifting her gaze from the passing landscape to his profile, she waited. A few minutes later, her jaw hung open.

"Roth! You didn't!"

"I just told you that I did, Sugar. And I'm not ashamed. He was begging to have his ass kicked. I simply obliged him. Just like I know you will if that delusional wife of his shows up again."

Dismissing his dig about her threat to Lucy, Autumn folded her arms across her middle, staring at him in disbelief. The day he'd confronted Russell was the same day he'd come home with custom bath salts, soap, and lotion to match the perfume he'd given her. She'd kissed and touched every inch of him that night, and he hadn't had so much as a scratch on him.

As a matter of fact, he'd been in such a jovial mood, he'd shared a bath with her, uncaring of the sweet floral scent from the salts he'd given her. They'd made love again in the water before falling into bed.

"Roth, it sounds like you beat that man to within an inch of his life, then came home to me with a smile on your face."

"I sure did." Beneath his thick facial hair, Autumn detected the presence of a smile almost as large as the one he'd worn that day.

Quirking one eyebrow, Autumn tilted her head to the side observing him.

"Hurting him made you happy?"

"Not particularly. But knowing I've protected you makes me downright giddy. He should count himself lucky Nick couldn't get leave on such short notice."

Autumn hadn't considered him pulling Nick into his criminal activities, but she should have. Despite the tension between them when she and Roth got together, Nick was still his best friend and her older brother. Shaking her head, she returned to staring at the landscape zipping past the window.

The warmth of Roth's palm resting on her thigh brought her gaze back to him.

"Don't worry, Sugar. I'm positive he got the message."

"Mhm. I'm not bailing you out of jail."

"Well, I guess it's a good thing I won't be needing you to."

Autumn's eyebrow climbed her forehead again. "Are you sure about that?"

Logically, she knew if Russell had intentions of pressing charges, the police would've already driven out to the Lazy Creek. It had been almost a week.

"I'm positive, Sugar. Even if the boys in blue come calling, I have a solid alibi. I'm on CCTV conducting business that day before I stopped by the little shop to pick up your smell good stuff."

Roth calling the scented bath salts and soaps *smell good* brought a wry smile to her face. There were times when he said some of the most old-fashioned things, but they sounded adorably country, and she loved it. She'd missed little things like that while living in Nevada and working in Las Vegas.

Opting to accept his confident reassurance, Autumn dropped her hand onto his, tangling their fingers together where they rested on her leg. Resolving not to give Russell another thought, she changed the subject to their upcoming trip.

Chapter Nineteen

The scent of the dense foliage filled Roth's nose, yet it still wasn't strong enough to block out the coppery aroma of freshly spilled blood. It was everywhere. On him. Around him. Splattered on the uniforms of his team members in various stages of injury, and in some cases, death. They shouldn't have been here. None of this should've happened.

Distantly, the sound of gunfire grew closer again. Yet the one sound he most wanted to hear. Needed to hear. Didn't reach his ears. The Blackhawk was quieter than older helicopters, but it didn't run completely silent. And Roth's ears were trained to detect the blades slapping against the wind. It wasn't coming.

One arm hung limply against his body and his left leg wasn't cooperating. Using his uninjured limb, he half crawled, half dragged himself closer to the harsh breathing of the nearest member of his unit. His own pain was inconsequential as he tried to reach Robbins.

Just as he got close enough to touch the young lieutenant, a whistling sound pierced the air right before the earth erupted less than twenty yards away. Throwing his body over Robbins', Roth tucked his head right before he was snatched into wakefulness.

Taking huge gulps of air, Roth stared, unseeing, with wide eyes. His body remained tense, coiled for the danger which now only existed in his dreams. Eventually, soft shushing noises penetrated the fog, pulling him the remainder of the way back to reality.

With his new focus, he realized the body he held tightly in his arms belonged to Autumn. It was his Sugar making the shushing sounds while delivering tentative strokes to his forearms. He held her so tightly it was the only place she could reach. Forcing his limbs to relax was a task accomplished in stages, but he was finally able to do it.

Once she had the space to maneuver, Autumn rolled to her back. The soft concern in her eyes and her gentle touch when she cupped his face sent a jolt of guilt lancing through him. Closing his eyes against the image, he dropped his head back onto the pillow.

"I'm sorry, Sugar." Opening his eyes again, he propped himself on one elbow leaning over her in the semi-darkness of the early morning. "I didn't hurt you did I?"

Stretching out his arm, Roth's fingertips grazed the base of the lamp on the nightstand. Light immediately illuminated her beautiful face. Visually scanning every part of her, he checked for the slightest hint of injury.

Autumn's soft digits closed around his wrist attempting to still his movements.

"I'm fine, Roth. You didn't hurt me." Sitting up, she peered into his eyes. "Are you okay? Do you want to talk about it?"

No. Roth absolutely didn't want to talk about it. As much healing as he'd done while working the Silver Creek Ranch, there was one time of year that was still difficult for him. It was the anniversary of his last mission. The date was emblazoned in his memory, not only because of the trauma and lives lost, but because it was also his birthday.

The scars on his shoulder and left leg no longer physically caused him pain, but he didn't need them to remind him. Each year, like clockwork, the closer it came to his birthday, he became a little more agitated. His sleep wasn't as restful. And it wasn't as if he'd gotten the most restful sleep in the past five years.

This year, he thought things might be different. Since the first night he spent with Autumn in his arms, he'd been able to sleep for more than four hours. He was actually resting with her beside him. But, even his Sugar's magic hadn't completely vanquished the demon. It still reared its head the day before his forty-third birthday.

"Roth?" Autumn's brow was creased with worry as she looked at him. "Do you want to talk about it?"

Remembering what he'd learned in therapy, Roth shifted until his back was resting against the headboard. Tugging her to lie against him, he released a resigned breath.

"Yeah, Sugar. I wanna talk about it."

Roth didn't fight the sigh which escaped when Autumn tucked her plush body into his side and rested her head on his chest. The arm she wrapped around his torso made him feel invincible. Like there was nothing he couldn't face with her next to him.

So, for the first time in recent memory, Roth told someone, other than the men who helped him heal, about the night that haunted his dreams. As he spoke, the heavy weight of guilt pressing down on his shoulders seemed to lighten. Once he was done, he realized he'd made it through the entire retelling without tensing up so stiffly he had to stop.

Short fingernails lightly scratched his beard-covered jaw before Autumn placed her palm against his face.

"Baby, I know you might have heard this before, but it wasn't your fault."

Rising, she shifted until she straddled his hips. Cupping his face in her hands, she pierced him with an expression filled with compassion, love, and confidence in her belief in what she was saying.

"You are an amazing man. I'm positive you were an excellent leader. I don't need to see your file to know those things. Because I know *you*. I know you wouldn't lead anyone into a situation where you didn't think you possessed the skills to be successful."

Roth wasn't sure he was ready to hear what she had to say. His eyes darted away from hers, but Autumn shifted her head until she was once again in his line of sight.

"I can't begin to imagine how what happened made you feel." Tracing the scar on his shoulder, she leaned forward to press a kiss to the area. "But what I do believe is that the Rothschild Stephens I know will always do whatever it takes to protect those he cares about."

Dropping his head until his forehead rested against hers, Roth let her words wash over him. He tucked them into his heart, rubbing them around like a balm. He had no idea how much he still needed to be assured he'd done everything he could to prepare and protect his men.

He couldn't count the times he'd done the same for the others who'd survived. Praising their efforts and convincing them they were in no way to blame for their brothers not making it home. While he'd meant every word he spoke to them, he didn't internalize them for himself. At least not completely.

However, when Autumn looked at him, with her eyes filled with love and conviction, he finally believed them. Holding her in his arms, he let his body speak his thanks for him, taking her lips in a kiss bursting with gratitude. And love. Because he loved Autumn Daley with every fiber of his being.

The thankful kisses transformed into more ardent gratitude which resulted in their bodies being tangled together as they brought one another to mutual completion. He was almost an hour late making his rounds and checking in with the hands. But, Roth didn't regret a thing.

The next day dawned, and for the first time since he'd left the military, the night of October 11th hadn't been plagued with the nightmares which had become a staple in his life before the morning of his October 12th birthday. As a matter of fact, it was off to an amazing start. Wetness and warmth engulfed the head of his cock.

His hands automatically sought out Autumn's hair, gripping it as she bobbed up and down, taking his length to the back of her throat before moving upward again.

"Fuck, Sugar."

Roth's moan was laced with the tortured pleasure coursing through him at her ministrations. Using her fingers to massage the portion of his shaft she couldn't fit into her mouth, Autumn sucked his cock like it was her favorite treat and she'd been denied access for far too long. The vibrations from her humming around his thickness created a pipeline taking him from hard to ramrod stiff.

"Shit! I'm gonna fucking come!"

He normally didn't make an announcement before shooting his load, but the swiftness of the feeling caught him off guard. The words tumbled from his lips a second before he yanked her off, pulling her upwards and rolling until he was on top with his cock poised at her molten hot entrance.

Kissing the pout from her plump lips, he slid inside her tight pussy. His tongue mimicked the probing movement of his length, not stopping until he was seated completely inside her velvet walls.

"Damn, baby. That's how to fucking wake a man up in the morning."

Autumn's thick thighs bracketed his hips as he thrust inside her. Her gasp was followed by a string of words that would make a preacher blush. Encouraging him to fuck her like he meant it, and to coat her insides with his cum, his Sugar rocked her hips into every thrust.

Grinning at her dirty mouth, Roth hooked an arm under her knee, changing the angle of his stroke. Her pants and filthy cheerleading morphed into wails of pleasure, making Roth work harder to bring her to the pinnacle.

"Come with me, baby. Cover my cock in your sweet cream. Give it to me."

Kissing a trail from her collarbone up her neck, Roth spoke directly into Autumn's ear. Her short nails dug into his flank and her channel clamped down on his tunneling thickness before it began to flutter. The release of her feminine juices was Roth's signal to let go. He stopped trying to control the tempo, allowing his hips to power into her, pushing his cock as far inside her as he could reach.

Stars burst behind his eyelids when he slammed them shut. The strength of his release sapped his strength, and he barely refrained from collapsing on top of her, giving her his full weight. Falling slightly to one side, he lowered her leg and gripped her hip, keeping them connected with his spent shaft pulsing inside her sweet heat.

Heavy breathing was the only sound breaking the silence in the bedroom. Their moans, sighs and dirty talk had been the soundtrack of their lovemaking. And now, the song had ended.

Not marking time, he didn't know how long they lay there before he finally withdrew his flaccid length. Despite her protests of him letting her take care of him on his birthday, he rose to prepare their shower before coming back to carry her into the bathroom.

They didn't linger in the shower. In a sudden burst of energy, Autumn rushed them through the process. So, any thoughts Roth had about another round were squashed. At least for the moment.

He didn't recall feeling such joy on his birthday in a very long time. Rolling with the feeling, he reminded her that as the birthday boy, he should have a choice when it came to what he wanted, including when they left the bed. Laughing, Autumn grabbed his right hand in both of hers, pulling him toward the stairs.

Before they entered the kitchen, he smelled the savory fragrance of bacon and sausage. When he stepped over the threshold, he saw the table set with platters of food in the center. His housekeeper, Amelia, normally cooked a small breakfast for them each morning, but this was reminiscent of a buffet.

In the seat at the head of the table was a navy-blue bag, with a silver bow affixed to the top. When he looked at Autumn, she was practically glowing. Yielding to the tug on his arm, he bent lower as she lifted on her toes, placing a quick peck on his lips.

"Happy birthday, baby."

"Thank you, sweetheart." Roth didn't have any other words, but those seemed to work for her.

It was good he hadn't been more exuberant in his thanks, because seconds later the sound of boots on hardwood garnered his attention. Thinking it was the foreman or a few of the hands, Roth turned toward the door to give them shit. Their presence explained the large quantity of food Amelia cooked.

Instead of the men he expected to see, honey-colored eyes that matched his own met his gaze.

"Pop?"

"Happy birthday, son."

His father stepped into the room, pulling Roth into a hug. Behind his father, were his mother and his younger brother Rhinehart. Once they'd all hugged him and wished him a happy birthday, Roth once again sought out Autumn.

"Sugar, what's all this?"

Chapter Twenty

Autumn was concerned maybe she pushed a little too much. She already had Roth's gift, but had decided at the last minute to see if his family could come over for breakfast. At the time, she didn't know why he was reluctant to celebrate his birthday. She just thought it was a nice compromise to having a large gathering.

After their talk the previous morning, she was a little concerned, but didn't call it off. It was time for him to stop isolating himself from the people who loved him. Birthday breakfast was a small step to reminding him he was still worthy of being celebrated.

Roth was staring at her waiting for an answer. Taking a deep breath, Autumn looked up at him, giving him a hopeful smile.

"It's birthday breakfast?"

Taking his hand in hers, she led him to the seat at the head of the table. It was his preferred spot because the only thing behind him was a wall, and it offered the best vantage point to see the entire room, including the doorways leading in and out. Lifting the gift bag from his seat, she placed it on the nearby island.

"You can open this later."

Following her example, his mother and Rhinehart also placed packages on the island. Butterflies beat their little wings in earnest in her belly. Autumn attempted to cover her nervousness with a smile, gesturing for everyone to sit.

"Son, I was looking at the grass in the southern pasture as we were driving in. Did you switch to Fescue?"

Nodding, Roth held out Autumn's chair, getting her seated before taking his own.

"Yes, sir. It grows faster and we don't have as many issues with bugs. I'll get the herd moved over as it starts to cool down more."

Autumn's nerves gradually settled as Roth, his father and his brother lapsed into a conversation about the ranch. Below the table, Mrs. Stephens squeezed the hand Autumn rested in her own lap. Looking up, she mirrored the older woman's smile.

As it turned out, her nervousness was for naught. Everything went off without a hitch. It was likely because the only time the focus was entirely on Roth was when it was time for him to open his presents. Rhinehart gave him a new pair of work gloves. Autumn had been away from ranching life for a long time, but she recognized the label and knew his brother had spent a pretty penny on the finely crafted gloves.

Before his parents gave him their gift, his father pulled out his phone and placed a call. Propping the device on the table between him and Roth, he pressed the icon to put the call on speaker. After two rings, Ryker's face appeared on the screen.

"Hey, Pop."

"Hey, son. I'm here with Roth and the rest of the family."

The butterflies in Autumn's stomach took flight again at his reference to them as *the rest of the family*. Somehow, she managed to keep from showing how the simple gesture affected her.

"Hey y'all. Happy birthday, Grouchy Smurf."

"Fu—. I mean, forget you. You aren't exactly the Jolly Green Giant yourself."

"Yeah, whatever." Ryker's voice was muffled for a second, and he turned his head to the side. A moment later, Ensley's smiling face was next to his.

"Happy birthday, Rothschild. And hey, Autumn. Hey, family."

Ensley's chipper greetings and obvious correction of Ryker's goading made Autumn smile wider. Seeing Ensley and hearing her voice gave Autumn a wistful twinge. She'd had a few random conversations with her Vegas friends, but she hadn't seen them since she'd begun her sabbatical. She didn't miss everything from her life there, but she did miss them.

"Okay, that's enough sweet talk, Darlin'. Roth, get your phone and check your messages."

Pulling his phone from his pocket, Roth's thick finger swiped across the screen. He stared at it for a few beats before he looked at his older brother.

"Are you serious?"

"Yep. I told you, that's never been the life for me. But, you wanted it, and I think it's where you're supposed to be."

Roth's thanks were issued around what sounded like a lump of emotion in his throat.

"Do we get to know what Rye gave you for your birthday?"

Rhinehart asked the question on Autumn's mind, but she wouldn't venture to ask. Roth looked at his brother before sweeping his gaze around the table, then back to the cellphone.

"He signed over his portion of the Lazy Creek."

"You're shittin' me." Rhinehart's outburst was immediately followed by the sound of his father smacking the back of his head.

"Watch your language."

"Sorry, Mama. Autumn."

"And Ensley." Ryker added to Rhinehart's list.

"Sorry, Ensley."

Autumn knew better than to do anything more than nod in acceptance. Mr. Stephens was old school. Men didn't curse in the presence of a lady.

Rubbing his head, Rhinehart looked at Roth. "If I'd known you'd accept it, I would've done that years ago." His voice trailed off mumbling about Ryker always upstaging him.

They ended the call with promises to see Ensley and Ryker soon. They were all traveling to Las Vegas for the wedding. Roth and Autumn would arrive that Monday, but his parents were traveling a week before them. Rhinehart had business. So, he wouldn't arrive until a couple of days prior.

Opening the remaining presents went quickly. His parents gifted Roth with a complete set of weatherproof notebooks. It was another perfect gift for him. He tended to carry a notebook in his back pocket all the time to jot down lists and other ranch related things. He rarely used the notes feature on his phone.

Autumn's gift was last to be opened. Her bottom lip wouldn't thank her for the way she nipped it between her teeth while she watched him pull the first item from the bag. His face stretched into a smile when he opened the monogrammed leather pouch and tipped out the pocket knife. The wood grain grip transitioned into black steel closer to the top.

Engraved in the wood were his initials. With practiced ease, Roth flicked out the blade, inspecting it. It appeared, once he was satisfied, he refolded the knife and placed it back into the leather pouch. One large hand cupped the base of Autumn's neck pulling her closer.

"Thank you, Sugar. I love it." A quick, but not chaste kiss was planted on her lips, causing heat to bloom in her cheeks.

Nodding toward the bag, nudged him. "You're welcome, but that's not all."

Roth's brow creased as he stared at the velvet box once he removed it from the bag. Flipping the lid open, he placed it on the table and lifted the item from the inside. From the outside, Autumn knew it looked like a pocket watch. However, when he pressed the button to open it, the true nature was revealed. It was a compass.

Using the tip of his fingers, he traced the words engraved inside the top cover. He didn't read them aloud. Roth simply peered at her, then gave her another kiss. This time, she wasn't as self-conscious. So, she was certain her entire face wasn't flushed.

Once all the presents were opened and Roth had passed the pocket knife around for his brother and father to see it, what Autumn planned for his birthday breakfast was pretty much done. There was no cake. No candles. Simply enjoying a meal, talking, and bestowing gifts. She did notice Roth didn't allow anyone to hold his compass.

They were forced to look at it while he held it in his hand. Afterwards, he attached the clip to his belt loop and tucked it into his pocket. The knife was attached to his belt. His other gifts were gathered and taken to his office.

Hand in hand, they walked his parents and brother out to their cars. As they drove away, the two of them moved to the porch. When Autumn went to sit on her own in one of the rocking chairs, Roth redirected her, settling her into his lap.

For a few moments, they sat there quietly absorbing the peacefulness of the late morning. Tucked into Roth's lap, she felt the steady thud of his heartbeat. His beard tickled her forehead each time he moved and held her close with one hand at her back while the other stroked her from hip to knee.

"Thank you, Sugar. This has been the best birthday I've had in...years."

Tilting her head to look up at him, Autumn kissed the base of his neck. "You're welcome. But the day isn't over. It's not even lunch time yet."

"As far as I'm concerned, we can sit right here with you on my lap until the moon comes up, and my statement will still be true. I don't need anything else for this day to be perfect."

"Well, it's your day. If all you want to do is sit here and watch the world go by. I'll sit with you."

Squeezing her in his arms, his reply was the kiss he placed on her forehead. They sat in silence for an unmeasured amount of time before Roth spoke again.

"Hey, Sugar."

"Hm?" Autumn slipped her arm around him, snuggling closer.

"About the inscription you put inside the compass cover."

Sitting up, she pierced him with a questioning gaze. "What about it?"

"It's really sweet, but there's something you need to know."

"What's that?"

"I love it. Because you gave it to me. And I'll keep it with me. Always. But I don't need a compass to help me find my way home."

Cupping her face in his hands, Roth gently kissed her lips. "Sugar, you're my home. So, if I ever need it, I'll use that compass to find you."

A puddle. Autumn was a literal puddle after Roth's declaration. He completely melted her with his words. Unable to form complete sentences, she simply pressed her lips to his, pouring all of her emotions into the kiss.

Chapter Twenty-One

Roth held up the glass figurine. It was an award of some kind Autumn had received from the company.

"Sugar, do you want this in here or was there something particular you wanted to do with it before it gets packed up?"

"You can put it in that box. There's no reason to separate things. I'll decide on a permanent solution when I get everything home."

Passing him a sheet of bubble wrap, Autumn continued gathering her other personal items.

"I kinda wish I'd done this when I left for my sabbatical."

Placing the glass statuette down on the bubble wrap, Roth carefully rolled it, making sure to cover the vulnerable edges.

"If you'd done this before you left, wouldn't you have essentially been telling them that you weren't coming back? Didn't you say you hadn't made up your mind at the time?"

Pausing in the act of removing a piece of framed art from the wall, Autumn worried her bottom lip.

"I hadn't officially, but deep down I knew."

Before Roth could delve further into her admission, there was a knock on the door. Not giving Autumn a chance to answer, the person knocking opened the door, stepping inside as if he had every right to barge into the space. Roth immediately placed the figurine aside to move closer to Autumn.

"I didn't invite you inside, Flint."

So, this was Flint Childers. Roth had heard about him, but seeing him in person solidified Roth's assessment. He was weak and insecure. Roth would hazard a guess it was partially due to his stature. Even with the obvious lifts he wore in his shoes, the top of his head barely reached Autumn's chin, which meant it didn't get as high as Roth's shoulder. Roth estimated he was barely five-foot-six inches, which was being generous.

Childers worked his mouth as if he planned to give Autumn a snappy reply. Then, he noticed Roth. Clamping his lips shut, his entire demeanor shifted from the falsely confident air of superiority he was cloaked in when he pushed the door open.

"My apologies. I thought I heard you say to come in."

The obvious lie and insincere apology were met with silence from Autumn. Roth was so fucking proud of the way she simply stared at Childers until he was uncomfortably shifting in his lifted loafers and clearing his throat. She didn't introduce Roth, or explain his presence. It wasn't any of the prick's business anyway. Finally, she either took pity on him or grew tired of his presence.

"Is there a reason you barged into my office, Flint?"

"Again." Childers cleared his throat. "I thought you called out for me to enter."

Autumn folded her arms across her middle. Childers immediately rushed to speak again.

"But that's neither here nor there." His eyes pinged between the Autumn to the mostly empty walls and the boxes resting on the now clear desk. "So, it's true. You're leaving Fortune?"

From the inflections in his voice, the casual observer would think Childers was genuinely concerned. But, having listened to Autumn's recounting of how her work life changed once the man joined her department, Roth was positive this little show was just that, a show.

When the two of them first entered the office earlier, it was to curious glances from some, and cheerful greetings from others. Autumn had only introduced him to a few people as they made their way to her office. The few people who were neither cheerful nor curiously staring solidified Roth's support of his decision to come in with her.

Despite asserting that she didn't need an emotional support person to join her when she went to quit her job, her fingers clamped around his, squeezing tighter when the time drew closer for the meeting she'd requested with her department manager and human resources.

Her plan was to turn in her resignation and complete the exit interview in one fell swoop. Waiting for her in her office, Roth had assembled the banker's boxes once Autumn's assistant brought them inside. Anything which obviously belonged to her—items with her name on them, he began assembling in neat groupings in preparation for her return.

"Yes, Flint. I'm leaving Fortune." Autumn didn't elaborate or attempt to assist Childers in getting to the point of his visit. Her posture projected her feelings concerning his presence very clearly.

"Well, uh. I'm uh. Sorry to see you go." Shifting again, he looked around the spacious room before he looked back at Autumn. "Before you officially call it quits, you didn't happen to look over the Royal Casino documents couriered over to you did you?"

Roth was already on alert, but hearing the slimy climber attempt to squeeze a little work out of his Sugar was a bridge too far.

"Get the fuck out."

Childers' startled jump would've been funny if Roth wasn't so focused on protecting Autumn.

"Pardon me? I don't see how this has anything to do with you." Showing he had bigger balls than Roth had given him credit for, Childers squared his shoulders and looked Roth in the eyes. "If you don't mind, I'd like to speak to Autumn privately, since this matter involves client confidentiality."

"I do mind. So, the answer is fuck no. Like I said. Get out."

Autumn's soft fingers on his bare forearm had Roth tilting his head slightly. While he wanted her to know he was listening, he kept his gaze locked on Childers.

"Roth, please. I can handle this."

A stiff nod was his reply. Keeping her hand on his arm, Autumn faced Childers.

"No, Flint. I didn't go over the documents. As you were well aware, until today, I was on sabbatical. And, as of an hour ago, I no longer work for Fortune Innovations. So, it is very much official. You'll have to find another attorney with corporate governance expertise to help you."

When she declined to help, Autumn was far more polite than Roth would've been. But, what she hadn't said was delivered loudly. She knew he attempted to sabotage her while simultaneously relying on her expertise behind the scenes.

The smile lifting Roth's lips was for more than one reason. He was proud of Autumn for holding to her boundaries. The other purpose for his nearly goofy grin was the two men who stood at the threshold to Autumn's office.

"Mr. Childers, we need you to come with us."

It was obvious from their attire that the men weren't regular building security. Comically rounded eyes threatened to pop from their sockets as Childers gaped at the two men.

"Come with you? For what? Who are you?"

One of the men reached into his breast pocket and pulled out a familiar leather identification folio, flipping it open. The gold shield opposite the official government agency photo was an exceptionally loud statement.

"Agents Rembrandt and Colder." Pocketing the ID, Agent Rembrandt stepped to the side and extended his arm. "It's in the best interest of all involved if you'd come with us quietly."

Childers visibly gulped. Wide spread fingers smoothed the front of his shirt from the knot in his tie down to the waistband of his belted slacks. Straightening his shoulders, Childers walked out. He and the agents made their way through the cubicles with Agent Rembrandt leading while Agent Colder brought up the rear.

As Roth observed people standing or coming to doorways to watch their progress through the office, his smirk grew to a toothy grin. While not as gratifying as when he cracked Russell's jaw and broke his arm, watching Childers' fall from grace was still very satisfying.

"Ow! What'd you poke me for, Sugar?"

Crossing to the door in three long strides, Autumn closed it, shutting them off from prying eyes and ears. Coming back toward him, she didn't stop until the tips of her business flats were touching the end of his square toed boots. When she folded her arms across her middle, he had to make a concerted effort to ignore the swell of her breasts visible courtesy of the opening in her dress shirt.

"Rothschild Stephens, what did you do?"

"What makes you think I did something?"

Tilting her head to one side, her expression projected the quintessential 'duh' she didn't say aloud. There was no point in denying it. He wasn't remotely ashamed.

Tugging at her arms, he unwrapped them, pulling her

closer. Folding her into his embrace, he dropped a kiss on the tip of her nose.

"All I did was make a couple of phone calls. An old team member now works in a different branch of the government."

"What branch, and how did you know there'd be anything to find?"

"The Department of Justice. And there's always something to find with those guys. You just have to get the right person on the trail."

"Is this going to blow back on Fortune?"

"Not if they cooperate. Considering the way they only escorted Childers out, tells me he was readily offered up, and his actions were disavowed."

Shaking her head, Autumn peered at him through her naturally thick lashes.

"I can't believe you..."

Kissing her pouty lips, Roth squeezed her tighter for a moment before relaxing his hold.

"I am who I am, Sugar. One day you'll realize there are no limits on what I'd do to protect you."

Roth nearly sighed at how good it felt when Autumn slid her hands up his chest before dipping her fingertips into the close-cropped hair at his nape. Lifting onto her toes, she pressed a far too chaste kiss to his lips.

"That is a dangerous prospect, Mr. Stephens. You should be careful saying such things."

"Nope. I said what I said." Reluctantly, he set her away from him with a tap on her lush ass. "Let's wrap things up so we can get out of here."

"Yes, sir." Putting an extra sway in her hips, she moved around the desk.

Roth resumed his task with practiced ease. Quickly, but carefully, filling the box before helping Autumn with the remainder of her things. As he stowed them in the back of her

SUV, he considered what could've happened if he'd been resistant to his mother's schemes and stayed away from the charity auction.

Is it possible he would still be where he was, helping the woman he loved close one chapter of her life so that they could begin another together? Or would he have still been roaming his ranch and never truly finding his home?

Epilogue

Roth adjusted the cuff of his shirt beneath the tuxedo jacket. What he really wanted to do was yank off the tie, rip the whole outfit off, redress in his jeans and plaid shirt and grab one of the horses from the barn. The coolness of the October day didn't do anything to make him feel less constricted standing between his brothers beneath the flower covered pergola.

Ryker's and Ensley's wedding was being held at Sunshine Ranch. It was where the two had their first official date. Or at least that's Ensley's story. Ryker said it was their second date. But those details didn't matter to Roth as he stared out into the crowd, locating Autumn's face. It was bad manners to say anyone was more beautiful than the bride on her wedding day, but his Sugar was by far the most stunning woman in attendance.

The setting sun cast a glow on her honey brown skin, making him want to lick every inch of her. Of course, since his current duties prevented him from acting on his desires, Roth just grumbled internally and counted the minutes until he could shed the restrictive clothing.

The reception was being held at the ranch as well. So once the happy couple said their I dos, and the obligatory photos were taken, Roth made his way to Autumn. She was standing in a small group next to Zaria and Andrei Antonov. He'd officially met both of them at the joint bachelor and bachelorette party a few days prior.

He recognized Andrei, not only from his days on the ice as a professional hockey player, but as one of Ryker's longtime friends. However, Roth had only heard about Zaria from the things Autumn told him about their time as members of the African American Women Association for Nevada Attorneys. She'd also been a part of Zaria's wedding earlier in the year.

Slipping an arm around her waist, he pressed a kiss to her cheek. Her soft fingers grasped his, and she smiled softly. He didn't interrupt the conversation, which was mainly between the two women. Nor did he attempt to engage Andrei in chit-chat. The guy wasn't much of a talker and it suited Roth just fine. When the crowd started moving toward the path lit by lanterns, Roth held Autumn back.

Curiosity coated her expression when she stared up at him.

"Hold on, Sugar. We haven't had a moment alone all day. If it wasn't Mama or your friends pulling you away, it was my brothers and Pop keeping me tied up. I just want to hold you and kiss you without an audience looking over our shoulders."

Slipping her arms around his waist, she snuggled close to him. "You know we're going to have the better part of a week where it's just the two of us, starting as soon as we leave here right?"

"Yeah, but you wouldn't begrudge a man a few moments of peace would you?"

It was a completely self-serving move, but he knew reminding her of his aversion to being around a group of people for extended periods of time would get him what he wanted. Although Ryker's and Ensley's wedding was relatively small and intimate, being surrounded by other people continuously was starting to wear on him.

"Take as long as you need, baby. I've got nothing but time." Resting her head on his chest, Autumn didn't say another word. She didn't have to. Simply allowing him to hold her was quite enough for Roth.

His thoughts drifted to their plans for the next week and a half. They were going to finish packing up her personal items, getting her condo ready for renters. Instead of having her vehicle shipped to Lone Star Ridge, they planned to drive the entire twenty-two hours, breaking it up over four days.

Roth was looking forward to having her all to himself with no distractions for either of them. He had a little surprise for her when they got close to Fort Hood in Killeen, Texas. However, before they reached Texas, they had another stop to make. One which would make his desires for their future abundantly plain. The velvet box was safely tucked into his go bag. He'd checked and rechecked the location so often, it was a wonder Autumn hadn't caught him.

Holding Autumn in his arms as dusk settled, Roth felt such a sense of completion. He would've been content to remain just as they were until it was socially acceptable to bid the bride and groom goodnight. However, he should've known their presence would be missed.

"There you two are!" His mother's voice penetrated their peace.

"Yes, ma'am. Here we are."

Roth didn't attempt to hide his feelings on them being discovered. Although, considering they were standing in the center of the aisle between the folding chairs, they weren't hidden very well.

"Don't you two even think about sneaking off." Shifting

her penetrating stare from Roth to Autumn, she smiled. "I told your mother we'd have to take some more photos. I'm so happy they were able to make it up. I wish Nicholas could've been here too. Then the whole gang could be together."

Releasing Autumn from his tight hold, Roth bit the inside of his jaw to keep the words inside. Although he and Nick weren't completely back to the way they were before, Roth knew his friend wasn't likely to show up to a wedding without being required to attend. To ease the sting, he offered her mild consolation.

"You know how things go with the military, Mama. They don't always line up the way we'd like."

"I know, son." Patting his arm, her expression was filled with warmth and empathy. "It's good that you're home now. Maybe Nicholas will retire and he can be home soon." Clapping her hands, her face brightened again. "Now, let's get to the party. No, dilly-dallying you two. And no sneaking off."

Spinning on her heel, she walked back towards the lake. Next to him, Autumn covered her mouth, but she wasn't successful in stifling her giggles. With a tug on her hand, he brought her curves back to his body.

"What's so funny?"

Mirth danced in her dark brown eyes as she looked up at him. Her fingers ghosted across his lips.

"I find your pouting amusing... And kinda cute."

Growling, Roth's hold on her tightened. "I'm a fully grown man. I don't pout and I'm not cute. I'm handsome."

"Uh-huh." Autumn's plump lips curved into a knowing smile. "Come on, handsome. Let's go show our faces. The sooner we do, the sooner we can go home."

Capturing her lips in a kiss filled with promise, Roth finally turned them in the direction of the party.

"Fine, Sugar. We can go be social for a little while."

With her hand in his, Roth was once again hit with the depth of his feelings for her. It didn't matter where they were, in his mind, he was already home because he was with Autumn.

The End

Up next in the series

Thanks for reading book one of the Silver Creek Ranch series! Up next is Healing Her Cowboys by Auriella Skye! Make sure you snag book six today!

Let's Keep in Touch!

Want to keep up with what's next and what's happening in my writing journey? Sign up for my monthly newsletter to get inside information, sneak peeks and excerpts!

https://sendfox.com/DarieMcCoy

Is the inside view from a newsletter not enough? To get more, you should join my Patreon. Tiers start as allow as $5 per month. Depending on your subscription level, you'll receive many perks from reading along as I write, up to receiving customized book boxes.

https://patreon.com/DarieMcCoy

Acknowledgments

First, thank you to Peyton Banks for including me in this wonderful collection. I had a great time writing Autumn and Roth, and it has been wonderful working with you. My sincere thanks to my Darlings, Delights, Decadents, and Divas. You ladies read my rough words, cheer me on, offer feedback to help me sharpen my pen. A special thanks to Michelle Jackson for lending me her military knowledge, answering my random questions to assist me in writing an authentic character. As always, I thank my writing partners, Brianna Q. Price and Niccoyan Zheng. Without your support, I don't think I could have grown as an author as quickly as I have. There's still work to do, and I couldn't be happier to have you on this journey with me. Last but not least, thank you to all the readers and everyone who lends me guidance and support throughout this author journey. You're amazing. I don't have enough words to show my gratitude.

About the Author

Darie McCoy is an independent author of contemporary, interracial, romantic suspense, and paranormal/shifter romance books. A reader first, she enjoys reading books across many genres although romance holds a special place in her heart. Her experience working in a STEM field offers her a unique perspective which she uses in each story she pens.

When she doesn't have her nose in a book or her fingers on the keyboard, Darie enjoys working in her vegetable garden. A serial hobbyist, she also enjoys knitting, sewing, baking and canning. One of her favorite treats to make is salted caramel popcorn. Amongst her friends, she's known to transport the sweet treat in large quantities to share whenever they get together.

Born and raised in the south, Darie stands by the staunchly held southern sentiments that the best tea is sweet tea and college football is life.

Also by Darie McCoy

Central Valley Pack Series

Chosen

Healed

Reclaimed

Frost Family Series

For Real

Sano's Queen (A Novella)

Christmas Candy

Draft Pick Series

Draft Pick Season I: Carver

Draft Pick Season II: Andrei

Draft Pick Season III: Denzel (Kindle Vella)

Draft Pick Season IV: Vitaly (Kindle Vella)

Other books/stories

Involuntary

Just Kiss Me (Part of Cupid's Kiss Anthology)

Toad: Sin City MC Oakland

Controlled Desire: Fall of Desire

The Glassmaker's Helper: The Getaway Chronicles

Construction Book Boyfriend (Book Boyfriend Series)